901223

The Bonnie Blue

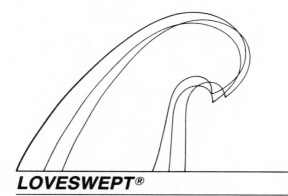

LOVESWEPT®

Joan Elliott Pickart
The Bonnie Blue

DOUBLEDAY

NEW YORK • LONDON • TORONTO • SYDNEY • AUCKLAND

LOVESWEPT ®

PUBLISHED BY DOUBLEDAY
a division of Bantam Doubleday Dell Publishing Group, Inc.
666 Fifth Avenue, New York, New York 10103

DOUBLEDAY and the portrayal of the anchor with a dolphin
and the word LOVESWEPT and the portrayal of the wave device
are trademarks of Bantam Doubleday Dell Publishing Group, Inc.

Library of Congress Cataloging-in-Publication Data
Pickart, Joan Elliott.
    The Bonnie Blue / by Joan Elliott Pickart.—1st hard-
cover ed.
        p.   cm.
    "Loveswept."
    I. Title.
PS3566.I275B6   1990
813'.54—dc20   90-33225
                                                        CIP

ISBN 0-385-41407-2

With special thanks to Elizabeth Barrett,
who went the extra mile

The Bonnie Blue

One

The saloon was crowded and noisy. It was Saturday night, payday, and the cowboys were out in force. The randy men had a number of pleasure palaces to choose from in Dodge City, Kansas, but the Silver Spur was by far the most popular. The Spur had the prettiest women—all ready, willing, and able—and the best piano player. The whiskey wasn't watered down and the card dealers were honest.

And the Silver Spur was fancy. A man felt important just walking through the swinging doors. Crystal chandeliers hung from the ceiling, their multitude of candles lighting the large main room as bright as day. The bar was a gleaming slab of highly polished mahogany, the mirror behind it reflecting the room into infinity. The women wore fancy dresses of velvet or taffeta with matching feathers in their hair. All of the Spur's fine trimmings had been brought in from the East, and the men of Dodge enjoyed the elegance, so different from the long hours they spent in the saddle, breathing in dust and the stink of cattle.

The Silver Spur was special, and it belonged to Mattie Muldoon.

Mattie stood at the top of the stairs and scrutinized the activity below. With a practiced and knowing eye, she could pick out the young cowboy who was close to having too much to drink; could pinpoint the strangers, and in one quick glance know who was potential trouble and who was there just for a good time.

But this Saturday night, she scanned the boisterous crowd looking for one man. He had to be there. She needed him to be there. Her heart beat wildly as she searched the room, hoping, hoping . . . Yes!

He was playing cards, his chair tilted back to lean against the wall. His Stetson was pushed up to reveal thick, black hair and sharp, handsome profile. His skin was bronzed by heritage and sun, his eyes as dark as the devil's. A gray western shirt stretched across his broad shoulders and chest, and Mattie knew well the rest of his rugged body. He was tall, more than six feet, with taut, hard muscles. Big and dark, magnificent and dangerous, he was a man all women fantasized about.

His name was Slade Ironbow.

Half Apache Indian, Slade had, in Mattie's opinion, the best attributes of his Indian father and white mother. He moved with the smooth, controlled grace of the Indian, and had a sixth sense that helped him survive a rough and wild country.

He stepped into the white man's world when he chose, and no one said more than once that he didn't belong there. A mere look from Slade's cold, obsidian eyes could pin a man in place. Those who pushed too far, who recklessly challenged him, felt the bullet from the gun that left Slade's holster with the speed of quicksilver.

Slade answered to no one, and Mattie never knew when

he might appear in Dodge. She suspected that he disappeared into the hills to spend time with his father's people, but he never told her. She never asked. Wild, contradictory rumors forever circulated about Slade, but she gave none of them credence. She'd believe only what he told her.

He'd returned to Dodge three days earlier, after being gone for two months. She'd greeted him without question, as though he'd never left. It had been like that for many years, and Mattie didn't expect it ever to change.

Slade Ironbow was thirty-two years old to Mattie's thirty-eight, and she loved him like a brother. Everyone believed they were lovers, when in actuality Slade was her best friend. And tonight she needed him more than she ever had before.

She slowly descended the stairs, nodding and smiling at those who greeted her. She forced herself not to rush to Slade's side and beg him to come upstairs, where they could be alone and she could pour out her heart to him.

Catching a glimpse of herself in the sparkling mirror over the bar, she studied her reflection, wondering if anyone could tell she was deeply distressed.

Her dark red hair was piled high on her head, with a few unruly tendrils curling along her slender neck. The emerald green of her silk dress was the exact shade of her eyes.

Her full breasts pushed above the low-cut, lace-edged bodice, enticing a second look from appreciative male eyes. The fact that it now took whalebone stays to give her breasts the lift they needed was nobody's business but her own. No one saw her naked body, for she was the owner of the Silver Spur now, and since Slade had come into her life, she no longer made her living by taking unwanted men into her bed.

Whenever any stranger pestered her, trying to buy her for an hour, or for the night, her bartender quickly and quietly informed him that she was Slade Ironbow's woman. The poor man would mumble his apologies and back away, disappearing into the crowd. No one, however, questioned Slade's enjoying the services of her girls. That was simply accepted as characteristic of an extremely virile man whom one woman would never satisfy. The charade with Slade served her well, and she was continually grateful for his compliance.

Mattie glanced at him again, wondering how long he and the three other men would play poker. Two of the men were wealthy ranchers; Mattie had seen them and Slade play through until dawn. Not tonight, she pleaded silently. Please, not tonight.

The other man was Doc Willis, who had been tending to the illnesses and injuries of the citizens of Dodge since before Mattie had come there more than twenty years ago. On any other night, she would have indulged in a moment's daydreaming about Doc Willis. She had loved him for years, and had kept that love a secret. She could never tell him.

With one last look at Slade, she turned away. The anxiety within her churned fiercely, and she could taste the metallic flavor of fear. Still, as she circulated through the growing crowd for the next hour, she managed to maintain her image of elegance, combined with an air of touch-me-not. Many a young cowboy followed her unhurried movements with his gaze, his heart and fantasies racing.

Mattie knew it the instant the two ranchers with Slade stood up, laughing and shaking their heads in defeat. A sob of relief nearly escaped her lips as the men ambled away, eyeing the girls who were still available. She walked toward Slade, instructing herself to move slowly, to smile.

"Well," she said, laying one hand on Slade's shoulder, "you scared those two off early tonight. Cleaned them out, by the looks of it. You and Doc seem to have won about the same amount."

"We did all right," Slade said.

His voice was dark and deep. One of Mattie's girls had said that Slade could undress a woman just by talking. But Mattie had also heard Slade's voice when it was as dangerous and cold as black ice.

"It's only fitting that I won tonight, Mattie," Doc said. "It's my birthday. I'm forty-seven years old today, and Lord knows I feel every one of those years."

"That's not old, Doc," Mattie said, smiling at the thin, good-looking man.

"It's getting there." He stood up. "I'm going to get us all a drink. We'll have a toast to me on my special day."

He walked away, and Slade began to stack his coins in front of him. "Trouble, Mattie?" he asked.

"How did you know?"

"I can tell."

She sat down next to him. "I need to talk to you, Slade, alone, as quickly as possible."

He nodded, then glanced up as Doc returned carrying three glasses.

"I didn't spill a drop," Doc said as he set the glasses on the table and sat down.

"Doc, I'm sorry," Mattie said. "I wasn't thinking. You shouldn't be paying for drinks on your birthday."

"True," Slade said. He picked up a few coins and tossed them into the pile in front of the doctor.

"I'll make the toast," Doc said, lifting his glass. Slade and Mattie lifted theirs too. "It's my birthday after all, so I can do as I please. I drink to you two, who I consider to be my closest . . . friends." He tipped his glass toward Slade, then slowly shifted his gaze to Mattie, looking directly into her green eyes. "To you, Mattie Muldoon."

"No," she said softly, "to you. It's your birthday, not mine. Happy birthday, Doc, and I hope you'll have many, many more."

Doc smiled. The trio sipped their whiskey, and Doc's gaze never left Mattie.

Slade glanced from Mattie to Doc, rolling the whiskey around on his tongue. Doc was in love with Mattie, he mused. He had suspected as much for a long time, but now was certain of it. Doc was making no attempt to conceal his feelings; love shone in his eyes. Mattie had to be able to see it, and Slade knew she would ignore it. Whatever she might feel for Doc Willis, she would never allow it to surface. She could never completely forgive herself for the life she'd led. Doc, to her, would always be out of her reach.

Slade swallowed more liquor. It took a helluva man, he realized, to do what Doc had done. He'd toasted Slade, calling him his friend, when he believed Slade was sleeping with the woman he loved. Doc Willis was a cut above the herd. And he and Mattie were still staring at each other.

The spell at the table was broken as a young cowboy rushed through the room, yelling Doc's name.

"There's been a helluva brawl at the Wooden Nickel," he gasped when he reached the table. "That fancy assistant doc you hired from back East said to come find you 'cause he's got more bloodied-up cowboys than he can handle. He's just a kid, that doc. You sure he knows what he's doin'?"

"He's older than you are, Tulsa," Doc said. He set his glass down and stood up. "You go on back and tell him I'm on my way."

"Yes, sir," Tulsa said, then took off at a run.

Doc smiled down at Mattie and Slade. "That ends my birthday celebration, but at least I shared it with good company while it lasted. I best get along and help patch up those roughnecks."

"Good night, Doc," Mattie said.

" 'Night," he said, then picked up his money and walked away.

Mattie clasped both hands around her glass and stared

into the amber liquid. "Don't say anything, Slade," she murmured. "I don't want to hear it. I saw how Doc looked at me. I know . . . I don't want to talk about it."

Slade took off his Stetson to run his hand through his hair, then settled the hat back on his head, pulling it low on his forehead so it cast a shadow over his features. He didn't say a word.

"Dear God, where is my mind?" Mattie exclaimed, pushing the glass away from her. "I have to talk to you, Slade. It's terribly important. I need your help and . . . Let's go upstairs."

Slade nodded and stood, scooping his money off the table. As Mattie started toward the stairs, Slade stopped at the bar and handed the money to the enormous black man behind it.

"I'll take care of it for you, Slade," the man said.

Slade made his way across the noisy, crowded room to where Mattie waited for him at the bottom of the wide staircase. With his arm circling her shoulders, they went up the stairs.

"Dammit, Abe," Clara, one of the saloon girls, said to the man behind the bar. "See that?"

"Mattie's got first claim on Slade Ironbow," Abe said. "You know that. Mattie is a very beautiful woman."

"I know it, Abe," Clara said, pouting, "but I don't have to like it. Slade hasn't come near me since he's been back. I wonder how long he'll be in Dodge this time?"

"There's no telling with Slade," Abe said, pouring a whiskey for a customer.

Clara sighed. "I know. You see him when you see him."

"Slade answers only to himself," Abe said. "Mattie understands that. There's nobody going to tame Slade Ironbow. Only a fool would try. You best go earn your keep, Clara."

"Yeah, I'm going," Clara muttered, and walked away with an exaggerated sway to her hips.

Abe watched as Mattie and Slade disappeared into Mattie's suite of rooms at the end of the hall upstairs.

"Nope," Abe said, wiping a wet spot off the gleaming bar, "nobody's going to tame Slade Ironbow."

Mattie and Slade passed through her small office, sparsely furnished with a desk, two chairs in front of it and a straight-backed one behind it, and a small safe against one wall. On the far side were hand-carved double doors, which Mattie opened with a key she took from her pocket.

Slade was one of the few people who had ever seen Mattie's living quarters, who knew they were much different from what most people expected of the owner of the Silver Spur. No bright, flashy colors or ornate furnishings decorated the sitting room or bedroom beyond.

Instead, Mattie had chosen pale rose and gray fabrics and wallpaper, and furniture made of shiny, dark mahogany. Small throw pillows edged in white eyelet decorated a rose velveteen settee. Elegant in their simplicity, evoking soothing calmness, the rooms could have been lifted from the home of any of the finest families in the country. Only one object was strangely out of place in the sitting room—a large, butter-soft leather chair. Slade's chair.

Mattie turned up the wicks on two oil lamps, then looked up to see Slade still standing just inside the closed doors.

"Drink?" she asked.

He shook his head, and crossed the room to his leather chair. Sitting in it, he placed his Stetson on a small table.

"Cigar?"

Again, Slade shook his head. He stretched out his long legs, crossed them at the ankle, then laced his hands loosely on his chest. Mattie began to pace the floor, and he watched her with half-closed eyes.

He presented the picture of a man totally relaxed, even almost asleep, but Mattie knew he was very much awake and following her every move. She also knew he wouldn't push her to speak, wouldn't insist that she tell him whatever was troubling her. Slade had the quiet patience of his Indian ancestors, and if Mattie chose to pace for an hour without saying a word, he would simply wait for an hour.

Mattie pressed her hands to her cold cheeks, drew a steadying breath, then sat down on the settee and looked at Slade. A minute ticked by in silence.

"Slade," she said finally, "you and I are the only ones who know how I came to own the Silver Spur ten years ago. You bought it, deeded it over to me, then advanced me the money to fix it up and make it the finest saloon in Dodge." Slade didn't move, nor acknowledge that he'd heard her. "I've paid you back every penny, and you know I'll be grateful to you for the rest of my life. I never understood why you chose me over all the other girls here. You've always just said you saw something in me that no one else did. Your friendship has been precious to me. I hope you realize that."

Slade didn't move or speak.

"Lord above," Mattie said, throwing up her hands, "there are times when your stoic Indian silence is maddening, Slade Ironbow."

He lifted one shoulder in a barely discernible shrug. "I know how you came to own the Spur, Mattie."

"All right, fine," she said, waving a dismissing hand. "What we've never talked about is how I came to be working here in the first place."

"That's not any of my business."

"Believe me, Slade, I'd prefer not to discuss it with you or anyone, but I have to now because I need your help." She paused. "I was raised by a drunken father back in Ohio. My mother ran off when I was just a little girl, and I was left with a bitter man who drowned his sorrows in a bottle. We lived in what was hardly more than a shack, and I cooked and cleaned and tried to please him. But he still drank, and when he did he beat me because I looked so much like my mother."

Slade remained silent, but Mattie saw a muscle jump along his jaw.

"I finally couldn't take it any longer," she went on, "and when a wagon train came through, I begged a family to take me with them. I offered to cook, do the wash, tend to the four children, if they'd give me food. They agreed, and I slipped away in the night to join them. I was barely sixteen then. It was a rough crossing, and a fever hit the wagon train. Two of the children died . . . It was horrible. When we got to Dodge, the family said they couldn't spare the food to take me farther. I was suddenly here, all alone, and terribly frightened."

She stopped speaking, as a shiver ripped through her, vivid pictures of her past flashing before her eyes. After a minute she had herself under control again, and lifted her chin as she continued.

"I met a young girl about my age, Maria Sanchez. She'd run away, too, from a life of poverty in Mexico. Maria and I lived in a tent at the edge of town and took in washing. Dodge was barely a town then, just mostly tents filled with trappers, gamblers, and prospectors hoping to strike it rich. Maria and I learned how to use a gun to protect ourselves from the men who came sniffing around our tent. Would you like a drink now?"

"No."

Mattie clasped her hands tightly in her lap and stared at her slender fingers. "Then I met a man. He was different from the others, so refined, a real gentleman. Or so I thought. He'd come calling and say I was the most beautiful girl he'd ever seen, an angel. I was swept off my feet. I'd tell Maria that everything was going to change, that I was going to marry him and I'd take her with me to my splendid new house."

She shook her head in self-disgust. "What a child I was. So naive and trusting, believing every word that man said to me. Then—then I knew I was carrying his child. I was thrilled, could hardly wait for him to come to the tent so I could tell him my glorious news."

Slade uncrossed his ankles, then crossed them in the opposite direction.

Mattie lifted her gaze from her hands to Slade's face. "He was furious. He slapped me hard across the face and told me I was nothing but trash. He'd never planned to marry me. He had only sweet-talked me to get me into his bed, and I'd ruined his good time by getting pregnant. He stalked out, and I never saw him again. I didn't know what to do. Maria was hysterical, so afraid we'd starve, and she didn't see how we were going to tend to a baby, too. Believe me, I didn't know, either, but it was my baby, and I was determined that nothing would happen to it. Oh, Slade, I don't know how to tell you why I need you so much right now without going through all this."

"Go on," he said quietly.

"Yes. Well, the months went by and I was sick a great deal of the time. It was cold and damp in the tent and I was trying to do my share of the laundry, but there wasn't enough food. I was so afraid for my baby. Maria started talking about working in one of the saloons, and I begged her not to. She was so young and innocent, I knew that life would kill her. My time was coming near, and I honestly didn't know how I was going to take proper care of my child."

She abruptly stood up and began pacing the room again.

"I had a baby girl," she said softly, stopping in front of Slade. "Maria helped with the birthing, and I held my beautiful baby girl in my arms. And I cried because I was so frightened, so afraid my baby would never survive. And then . . . then he came. Jed Colten. He was with a wagon train on its way to Texas. He'd pulled out of the train in Dodge because his wife Bonnie was expecting a baby and was very sick. My own child was a week old when Mr. Colten came to see me. He'd heard about me, he said, and wanted to talk. He was young and strong, and as he spoke, he started crying. His wife had given birth to a girl, but the baby had died. Bonnie was in a fever, and didn't know her baby was dead. Slade, Jed Colten was the kindest, gentlest man I'd ever met. His Bonnie was his life, his reason for living."

Unnoticed tears spilled onto Mattie's cheeks as she sank back down on the settee. "He said it would break his wife's heart when she learned their baby had died. He swore on all that was holy that he'd give my daughter a good life, treat her as his own if I'd let him. No one would ever know, especially Bonnie, that the child wasn't a Colten. I knew in my heart that I owed my baby a chance at a life better than I could provide for her. Jed wanted to give me money, but I refused. My only demand was that he take Maria with him, get her out of Dodge, let her be a part of his household. I swore I would never try to see my daughter if he'd take Maria. Slade, I—I gave my baby to Jed Colten. Do you hate me for that?"

"No."

"I gave my baby away!"

Slade straightened in the chair and leaned forward, resting his elbows on his knees.

"No," he said, looking directly at her, "you gave your baby a *chance.* That took more courage and love than keeping her."

"Thank you," Mattie said, dashing her tears away. "Mr. Colten took the baby and Maria. My life got worse in Dodge, until I was nearly starving. I just gave up and went to work at the Silver Spur. It was rough, sometimes frightening. Fistfights—gunfights every night, and the other women were so hard, so completely without hope. I just blanked my mind and did what I had to do. Each day, each night, I thought about my daughter.

"Over the years, Maria has sent me letters whenever she knew of someone who was coming to Dodge City. She felt I'd saved her life, and to repay me she kept me informed about my child. Jed Colten did well in Texas. He homesteaded, then bought up neighboring land as people gave up on it. He named his spread the Bonnie Blue. They named my daughter Becca. When Becca was six, Bonnie died of pneumonia. Maria assured me that the Bonnie Blue was a wonderful ranch, that Jed Colten was devoted to Becca, and that with Maria's help he would raise her. He never remarried, because his only love had been Bonnie, and he centered his attention on Becca. To him, she was his own daughter, and I found peace in that."

"You should," Slade said. "You did the right thing, Mattie."

"But, Slade, now there's trouble, terrible trouble, and I need your help. I've had a letter from Maria. Jed Colten was killed two months ago when his horse threw him. Becca has just turned twenty-one and inherited the Bonnie Blue. But another rancher, Henry Folger, is trying to get the ranch. Maria said he offered to marry Becca, but Becca refused. Folger was livid, and threatened to get the Bonnie Blue any way he could. Maria is frightened for Becca, and Becca is determined to stand her ground and run the ranch herself. Oh, Slade, I'm so afraid for my baby."

"Where's the Bonnie Blue?" he asked.

"In the northwest section of the Texas Panhandle, just over the border below Oklahoma. Three, maybe four days' hard ride from here."

Slade planted his large hands on his thighs and pushed himself to his feet. "I'll leave at dawn."

Mattie jumped up and grasped his hands, tears filling her eyes again.

"You'll help her? You'll help Becca?" she asked, a sob choking her voice.

"You knew I would."

"It could be dangerous, Slade. It doesn't sound like Henry Folger will take kindly to anyone getting in his way. I hate to ask this of you, but I didn't know where else to turn."

"I'm the only one you should have come to with this. You know that, too."

"Becca mustn't know about me."

"I understand."

"You can tell Maria who you are but . . . how will you explain yourself to Becca?"

"I'll think of something once I get there and see the situation. Try not to worry. I'll send word to you when I can."

Mattie wrapped her arms around his waist and leaned her head on his chest. He embraced her, holding her tightly to him.

"There aren't words to thank you," she said, sobbing openly. "I love you, my friend. How can I ever repay you?"

He gripped her upper arms and set her away from him. "You can stop crying. I've never seen you with tears in your eyes before, Mattie, and I don't know what to do with a crying woman."

She managed a small smile and swept the tears from her cheeks. "There. No more tears. But, Slade, please be careful. Maria says that Henry Folger is rich and powerful, and will stop at nothing to get the Bonnie Blue. I'll never forgive myself if anything happens to you. If it weren't for Becca being in danger . . . Oh, promise me you'll be on your guard."

He picked his Stetson up. "I will," he said as he settled his hat low on his forehead. "Don't expect to hear from me right off. Put your mind on something else if you can." He started toward the door. "For instance, you could think about Doc Willis and the fact that he's in love with you. And that maybe it's time Doc knew that you and I aren't doing up here what everyone thinks we are."

"Slade, don't be ridiculous. Doc is a fine, upstanding citizen of Dodge City."

Slade put his hand on the doorknob, then turned to look at her. "So are you."

"No, I'm not. I don't want to talk about Doc. My thoughts will be with you and Becca. My prayers, too. Please be—"

"Careful. I always am. I'm going to get some sleep. I've got a hard ride ahead of me. Good night."

"Good night, and I thank you with all my heart."

Slade nodded, then left the room, closing the door with a quiet click.

Mattie's trembling legs refused to hold her for another moment, and she sank onto the leather chair. She could feel the comforting warmth from Slade's body. As another sob rose in her throat, she gave up the battle against her emotions. It had been many years since she'd cried, and now she seemed unable to stop the flow of tears.

She covered her face with her hands and wept.

Two

Slade slowly walked down the stairs and out of the Silver Spur. Clara stamped her foot in a fit of temper, causing Abe to chuckle and shake his head.

Outside, Slade glanced around instinctively to take stock of the mood of the city. Saturday nights were usually wild and reckless. The numerous saloons were ablaze with light, music and raucous laughter pouring out of them in waves.

The sheriff and all his deputies would be keeping careful watch, Slade knew. Sunday morning, cowboys would be waking with aching heads and foggy memories. Some would be battered and bruised, others would find themselves in jail and wonder how they'd gotten there.

The church would be packed for the weekly service, and the preacher would forcefully denounce the evils of drink and the sins of the flesh. Monday would bring a return of the work routine, then next Saturday night the process would begin all over again.

Slade strode along the weatherworn wooden planks laid as sidewalks above the dusty streets, Becca Colten's name ringing in his mind. Mattie's daughter. Mattie's secret for twenty-one years. What it must have taken, he thought, for her to give up her baby. She was strong, his Mattie, and her heart and soul were purer than those of the many hypocrites who'd show up at church the next morning.

He'd sensed the goodness in Mattie the first time he'd seen her, and had set about to make a better life for her. Mattie was one of the few people he allowed to get close to him. He'd never touched her as a lover. She was his friend, pure and simple.

As Slade strolled toward the hotel he stayed in whenever he was in town, he saw Doc Willis sitting on the bench in front of his office on the other side of the street. Slade crossed the street, kicking up dust, and settled onto the bench next to the doctor. Several minutes passed in silence.

"You're turning in early," Doc finally said.

"Yep."

"I just fixed up some battered cowpokes. God knows why, but those poor buzzards inspired me to take stock of my life. You ever do that, Slade? You ever sit on a bench and take stock of your life?"

"No."

"Well, maybe it's because it's my birthday. A man sometimes takes a hard look at himself on his birthday."

"Sometimes."

"Can't say I liked what I came up with."

"No?"

"No. I'm a lonely man, Slade. I want a wife, a family, before I'm too old to have one."

"Reasonable."

"No, it's not, because the woman I love belongs to someone else. Can't see myself settling for less."

"No."

Doc chuckled. "Carrying on a conversation with you is like talking to a board. Never met a man who can say so much with so few words the way you do. I suppose that's the Indian part of you coming through."

"Yep."

"What would you do, Slade, if the woman you loved belonged to another man? Not married, mind you. He's just staked his claim on her."

"Shoot him."

Doc shook his head. "Oh, hell."

"You asked."

"All right. Suppose this man you're planning on shooting is a friend of yours? What then?"

"Depends on how much I want her."

"Love her. There's a big difference between wanting and loving."

"I wouldn't know."

"You've never been in love?"

"No."

"You ever killed a man because you wanted his woman?"

"No."

"I couldn't do it."

"I know you couldn't, Doc. And it isn't even necessary. Mattie and I aren't lovers, never have been. You are now the only other person who knows that. Because everyone believes she's mine, men stay away from her. That's what she wants. I know you love her; I've known for a long time. I figure you're about to do something about it. Don't feel you have to shoot me, though."

Doc shook his head again.

"I can't believe this."

"Believe it."

"Slade, before you go back to your short Indian answers, could you tell me how I'm going to convince Mattie Muldoon to marry me? I'm not even sure she likes me much."

"She likes you."

"She does?"

"Yes. She likes you just fine. The problem, Doc, is that Mattie doesn't carry a real high opinion of herself. With you being a respectable doctor, a high-class citizen and all . . ." Slade's voice trailed off, and he shrugged.

"Lord, when you start talking, you really have things to say. Mattie doesn't think she's good enough for me? That's pure horse manure. I'd be the proudest man alive to have her as my wife."

"Tell her."

"Oh, Lord," Doc said, looking to the heavens.

"Doc, I'm riding out at dawn to tend to some business. Mattie's a bit upset about a private matter, and I'd appreciate your checking on her for me. When I'm a day's ride out and she can't come gun me down, tell her I told you the truth about her and me. The rest is up to you."

"You've said more tonight than you've said in the past ten years."

Slade got to his feet. "You'll wait ten more years to hear as much again. I'm all worn out. 'Night, Doc."

"Thank you, Slade. I count myself lucky to have you for a friend. You realize, don't you, that if I start courting Mattie while you're gone, everyone will expect you to come back and shoot me dead as a post?"

Slade chuckled. "That they will. There will be lots of disappointed folks around here. They do enjoy a good shooting. Do you mind if I get some sleep now?"

"Oh, sorry. Good night, Slade, and thanks again."

"Happy birthday," Slade said, then disappeared silently into the darkness.

"It wasn't a happy birthday," Doc said to no one, a smile creeping onto his face, "until now."

A half-day's ride out of Dodge, Slade left the well-traveled road and headed for the backcountry. He had no desire to meet up with the various travelers, salesmen, down-on-their-luck cowboys, and thieves who traversed the better-known thoroughfares. He always felt more comfortable finding his way in uncharted territory. There his sixth sense would warn him of any danger from man or beast or terrain.

Blanking his mind of thought, beyond listening for potential trouble, he rode tirelessly. His horse, a big, black stallion, knew every nuance of his master's body, and the two moved nearly as one entity, emanating gracefulness and seemingly unending power and strength. The wind accompanied them, as though realizing this man and beast were kin, as fleet and wild as itself.

For Slade it was a cleansing time away from the noise and activity of Dodge City. He filled his lungs with the whipping wind and pushed on. At dusk he found a secluded spot to make camp. After tending to the needs of his horse, he stripped bare and plunged into a swirling stream that washed away the dust of his hard ride.

His food was simple but nourishing, and included pecans from the many trees that grew near the water. Tall oak and elm trees stood like proud sentries at the edge of the stark desert beyond, where the water couldn't reach.

When Slade slept, he slept light, his gun close to his side. At dawn he was up, cleanly shaven, dressed, fed, and saddling his horse, who pranced in anticipation of another day racing the wind.

He continued south, and could often see in the distance railroad tracks snaking across the land. Soon, he knew, the country would meet itself coming and going. What had been wild, would be tamed; what had been undiscovered, found. Among the men who ventured far into the West, some were pure of heart, carrying hopes and dreams for a better life. Others were simply greedy, not caring about the land or its natural gifts as they took all they could for themselves, then moved on.

It was a time of change, and Slade accepted that, as did his father's people. The Indians had fought bravely to hold what had always been theirs. Fought and lost. Most of the tribes now lived on reservations, scratching out an existence far different from their fathers' before them.

As time passed, though, Indians were slowly gaining nervous acceptance in the towns, where they bought supplies. In his many travels, Slade had seen Indian children sitting next to white in small schoolhouses; seen on occasion a white man tip his hat to a young Indian woman in the marketplace.

Perhaps, his father often said, there would be a time of total peace in the country, with all people living side by side with no thought of color, creed, or heritage. Perhaps, Slade always answered, but he felt in his heart that it would never come to be.

Man was a creature of fear, and what he didn't understand he struck out at. Until that changed, there would be dissension. But for now, at least, a tentative calm held as everyone struggled to survive.

In the late afternoon, three days after leaving Dodge, Slade sat on his horse on a rise high above the sprawling Bonnie Blue ranch.

Early in the day he'd met an old prospector with no particular destination in mind who was riding along on a mule. The man knew the Bonnie Blue and told Slade exactly how to find it. It was the finest spread around, stretching for miles in every direction, the old man had said, though Lord knew what was to become of it with Jed Colten dead.

"Second best is Folger's place," the man said. "Four Aces, he calls it." He spat tobacco juice on the ground. "Big spread, right next to the Bonnie Blue. Folger wants Colten's land real bad, I hear. Put them two ranches together, he'd be takin' a big bite out of Texas soil. Can't say I know how it's all goin' to end up, but I'm headin' out. Texas is gettin' too crowded for me."

Slade had nodded, then pressed on to find the Colten ranch. Gazing at it at last, he knew it was all he had heard about it.

Cattle covered the rich, rolling, checkerboard land. Some acreage was lush, with alfalfa growing tall and thick. Other sections had been well grazed, and were left alone now to replenish their bounty. Dozens of horses nibbled grass and raced in large fenced-off enclosures. In the distance were buildings—a huge barn, sheds, a bunkhouse, and a sprawling ranch house.

The Bonnie Blue was a fine spread, he thought, one of the best he'd seen. Windmills were pumping the precious water needed to keep it all going. He could see cowboys leading horses into the barn; smoke curled up from the chimneys of the bunkhouse and ranch house, indicating supper was being prepared. A sense of peace enveloped the scene, a sense of man and nature working together to create harmony.

But just how peaceful was it? Slade wondered. Had Maria Sanchez panicked when she'd sent the message to Mattie? Did Becca Colten intend to marry Henry Folger and merge the two ranches, but put the man through his paces first?

The Bonnie Blue was enormous. That meant money. Jed Colten had adored his adopted daughter, treated her as his own flesh and blood. That could have produced one very pampered and spoiled young lady, whose act of defiance was nothing more than a display of female dramatics. Or was Becca really in danger, as Mattie feared?

There was, Slade thought dryly, only one way to find out, and sitting up there on a hill admiring the Bonnie Blue wasn't going to get him the answers he needed.

He swung his horse around and made his way back

down the rise, deciding to approach the ranch from the front. If he was riding into a hornet's nest, he preferred to face it head-on. If nothing was really wrong, he'd be on his way before heavy darkness fell.

Nearly an hour later, Slade had made his way down, then around the miles of fenced land, which were even richer and more fertile at close view. At last he followed a winding dirt road that led to the gleaming white house. He walked his horse at an easy pace, his gaze flicking in all directions. He saw no one.

Stopping in front of the house, he saw it was well cared for. Two stories high and painted a sparkling white, it had a sweeping front porch, reminding him of a planta-tion house he'd seen when traveling through the South a few years earlier. As he prepared to dismount, the front door burst open.

Slade stiffened when he saw a rifle pointed at his chest. And holding that rifle, stepping slowly onto the porch, was one of the most beautiful women he'd ever seen.

This was Becca. She was dressed in mourning black, and her auburn hair, darker than Mattie's, was pulled back. She'd inherited Mattie's green eyes and creamy complexion, but she wasn't Mattie. She was Becca, uniquely herself. Tall and full-breasted, with a tiny waist and slim hips. Her features were delicate and lovely; her lips inspired dreams of stolen kisses on moonlit nights. Yes, Becca Colten was beautiful, and at the moment she was ready to shoot him dead.

"Ma'am," he said, touching two fingers to the brim of his Stetson.

"Just turn around and leave, mister," she said. "I know Folger sent you. I don't have any idea what his plan is this time, but you can tell him that the Bonnie Blue is not for sale, and neither am I. Now, move it."

"Before you pull that trigger," Slade said, "I might just mention that I don't know anyone named Folger."

"Who are you?"

Before Slade could reply, the sound of rapidly approaching horses snapped Becca's head up. Four riders galloped up to the house, and Becca shifted the rifle from Slade to them. Slade sat perfectly still, giving the appearance of being completely relaxed. The men pulled their horses to a stop, glanced at Slade, then looked at Becca.

"Howdy, ma'am," one said. "Just came checking on you for Mr. Folger. He's mighty concerned about you, you know, being here on your own."

"In a pig's eye," Becca said. "You're not welcome on Bonnie Blue land, any of you, including Folger. You tell him that—again—and maybe one of these days it will sink into his thick skull."

Slade watched her with surprise and admiration. Her eyes glittered with anger, and her breasts rose and fell rapidly. He'd seen her pale as the men approached, but she was standing her ground. The trembling of the rifle was barely discernible. Becca Colten wasn't playing games. This was no show of female dramatics. She was most definitely in trouble.

"Now, now, Miss Colten," the man said, almost sneering, "that ain't real neighborly of you. Mr. Folger's just worried about you, is all. It's bad enough your pa had the fall that killed him, and now we hear tell over at Four Aces your foreman met with a real unfortunate accident. Broke his leg, is how the story goes. So, Mr. Folger, being a gentleman and all, sent me to take his place. I brought some of my boys along to help out. My name is Casey, and I'm at your service, ma'am. Your new foreman."

"She already *has* a new foreman," Slade said quietly, shifting his gaze to the four men.

They turned their heads around to look at him. Becca stared at him, too, her eyes wide.

"Who in the hell are you?" Casey asked.

"Just told you," Slade said. "The foreman."

"You got a name?"

"Yep."

"So?" Casey said. "What is it?"

"Miss Colten knows who I am," Slade said. "You don't need to."

"Who is this man?" Casey asked Becca. "We didn't hear nothin' about your hirin' a new foreman."

"Because it's none of your business," Becca said. "Now, turn those horses around and get off my land."

"Not 'til we got a name to take back to Folger," Casey said. "He's going to want to know who you brought in."

"Ironbow," Slade said. "Slade Ironbow. I'm only telling you because you're making Miss Colten and me late for supper."

"Holy hell, Casey," one of the other men whispered. "Did you hear him? He's Slade Ironbow. I've heard about him. All kinds of things. Let's get the hell out of here."

"I ain't afraid of you, Ironbow!" Casey yelled.

Slade shrugged. "You should be, but it's up to you. You can leave upright in the saddle, or slung over it. Take your pick."

"On your way," Becca said, tightening her hold on the rifle.

Casey hesitated, glaring at Slade, then looked back at Becca.

"Folger isn't going to like this," he said, "your bringin' in a fast gun. Folger's been keeping this nice and friendly, but you're changin' the rules."

"Folger's idea of friendly doesn't match mine," she said. "Nothing he's done has come close to being friendly. Don't come back, any of you. I'll say this one last time. The Bonnie Blue is not for sale, and neither am I. Go!"

"Now," Slade added quietly.

With a muttered curse, Casey swung his horse around and galloped off, the others right behind him. Becca slowly lowered the rifle, drew in a shuddering breath as she watched them leave in the billowing dust, then swallowed hard.

Slade waited, not moving, for her to regain control. She had, he realized, momentarily forgotten he was there as the shock of the encounter with Folger's men took its toll. She suddenly seemed fragile, vulnerable, and he fought the urge to go to her and pull her into his arms, to tell her no harm would come to her because he was with her now.

Nothing, he vowed, was going to happen to the Bonnie Blue or to Becca Colten. He'd protect her. Tears should never cloud her eyes as they did now; her lower lip shouldn't tremble with fear and despair. No, he'd take care—

Slade drew himself up short, stunned by his thoughts. What he was thinking, and feeling, had nothing to do with his friendship with Mattie. Becca was rousing powerful emotions in him, not because she needed his help, but because she was a beautiful, desirable woman. And those powerful emotions threatened the control he always maintained.

"Could I get off this horse now?" he asked gruffly. "Assuming you've decided not to shoot me."

Becca blinked, then spun around to face him. She'd unconsciously cradled the rifle, pointing it harmlessly at the ground. "What? Oh, yes, of course . . ."

Slade swung from the saddle in a smooth, graceful motion. The reins in one hand, he shoved his Stetson up with his thumb and gazed at her. Their eyes met, and he felt a coil of heat tighten deep within him.

Damn, he thought, what was it about this woman? She was turning him inside out just looking at him. He was hungry, that was it. He'd had a long day in the saddle, and a decent meal and a night's sleep would chase away these unsettling reactions to her.

"Who are you?" she asked. "I know your name is Slade

Ironbow, and Folger's men said you were a fast gun. They were obviously intimidated by you. What are you doing here on the Bonnie Blue, Mr. Ironbow?" She lifted her chin, steadily holding his gaze.

Well, Slade thought dryly, Miss Colten was definitely back in control. "Hear tell it, I'm your new foreman."

"Look, Mr. Ironbow—"

"Slade."

"I believe, sir," she said stiffly, "that you owe me an explanation for your presence on the Bonnie Blue."

He shook his head. "Now you're getting all snooty. You do change moods right quickly, Miss Colten."

"Answer my question," Becca said, her voice rising. "How do I know this whole thing wasn't staged? How do I know you don't really work for Henry Folger, and this isn't a carefully concocted plan of his? Just how do I know that, Mr. Ironbow?"

"Slade."

Anger flashed in her eyes once more. "Damn you."

A smile tugged at the corner of Slade's mouth, then was gone. "Now you're swearing like a drunken cowboy. You're an amazing woman, Miss Colten." She really was, he thought. She was fire and fury one minute, then looked like a frightened fawn the next. She'd be a lot to handle for any man who tried to stake a claim on her, make her his.

"I need to see to my horse," he said, cutting off his musings before they went down the wrong road again. "We've had a long, hard ride. Then, if you can spare me a plate of supper, I'll answer your questions."

Before Becca could reply, a young cowboy raced around the side of the house. He pulled up short when he saw Slade.

"Miss Becca?" he asked, his gaze darting back and forth between her and Slade. "Are you all right? I saw dust from the road. Were Folger's men here?"

"Yes, they were," Becca said, "but I'm fine. Bucky, would you please see to Mr. Ironbow's horse? Mr. Ironbow and I have things to discuss."

"Yes, ma'am," Bucky said. He approached Slade cautiously. "I'll feed and water him, brush him down real good. Fine animal, sir. A beauty."

Slade lifted his saddlebags off the horse and flung them over one shoulder, then handed the reins to Bucky.

"Horse got a name?" Bucky asked.

"No," Slade said.

"Oh. Well, I'll tend to him just fine. Good evening, Miss Becca."

"Thank you, Bucky," she said, watching as he led the horse away. Then she switched her gaze back to Slade.

"I need to wash up," he said, and added, "before supper."

Her mouth tightened. "All right, Mr. Ironbow, you win. For now. There's a pump around back where you can wash up. Come into the house through the kitchen door when you're finished. I'll tell Maria to set an extra place for supper. During supper—not after—I'll expect you to answer my questions."

He nodded and started away. "Slade," he said over his shoulder without breaking his long-legged stride.

Becca glared at his retreating back, then went into the house, slamming the door behind her. After setting the rifle back in a rack that held six others, she strode down the long hallway to the kitchen.

Was she making a mistake by letting Slade Ironbow into her home? she asked herself. What if he was one of Folger's men? Casey and the others could have pretended to be frightened of him. Mr. Ironbow had better have some straight answers for her. But how was she to know if he was telling her the truth? Oh, saints above, she was about to have supper with a gunfighter!

She entered the kitchen to find Maria looking out the window.

"Maria, would you please set an extra place for supper? Mr. Ironbow will be joining me."

Maria glanced at Becca, then turned back to the window. She was a short, plump woman, with dark hair pulled into a neat bun, and warm, expressive brown eyes. While not beautiful, Maria had an aura about her that made one immediately feel comfortable with her.

"Is that your Mr. Ironbow washing up there?" Maria asked. "Mercy, mercy, mercy, that is one fine-looking man. He took his shirt off to wash up and his chest, his back, his arms . . . Muscles in all the right places and skin like polished copper. Mercy, mercy—"

"Maria, for heaven's sake," Becca said, "you've seen many a man wash up for supper."

"Not one like that," Maria said, her gaze still riveted on Slade. "Where'd he come from, Becca?"

"I don't know." Do not look out that window, Becca Colten, she told herself firmly. "I intend to get answers to my questions over supper." She moved closer to Maria, and of its own volition, it seemed, her gaze was drawn to the window. "Oh. Oh, my," she said softly.

Slade was just reaching for his shirt, and the muscles in his back rippled beneath taut, bronzed skin. He turned to shrug into the dark shirt, and Becca's breath caught in her throat as she saw the moist, black hair on his chest. A funny flutter danced along her spine; her cheeks warmed.

"Got some Indian in him by the looks of him," Maria said. "Name sounds Indian. But he's part white, too, 'cause he's got hair on his chest. Oh, he is a handsome devil, that one."

"He's a gunfighter," Becca said.

Maria shrugged. "I knew that right off. You can tell from the way he wears that gun low on his hips and tied down. You don't know where he came from, or why he's here?"

"No," Becca said, "but I'll know before supper is over. Four of Folger's men were here. Slade—Mr. Ironbow told them he was my new foreman. As soon as he said his name, the Four Aces men hightailed it down the road."

Maria laughed. "I'm sorry I missed seeing that. So, your Slade has a reputation, does he?"

"Maria, he's not mine." Becca spun around. "I'll wash up in my room. Please ask Mr. Ironbow to meet me in the dining room."

"That I will," Maria said as Becca stalked out of the kitchen. "But if I don't quit gawking at the man, there won't be any supper to serve up."

As Maria returned to the large wood-burning stove, the back door opened and Slade walked in, carrying his Stetson and saddlebags. He set them on the floor next to the door. Maria turned and smiled at him.

"Welcome to the Bonnie Blue, Mr. Ironbow. I'm Maria Sanchez, the housekeeper."

"It's Slade."

"Well, then, you call me Maria, Slade. Supper will be on in just a few minutes. Becca said to go into the dining room. It's down the hall, first door on the right."

"Where's Becca?"

"In her room washing up."

Slade nodded and crossed the kitchen to stand in front of Maria. "Mattie sent me," he said quietly.

"Oh, praise the Lord," Maria said, covering her heart with her hand. "We're in trouble here, Slade. Bad trouble. I hated to upset Mattie, but I didn't know what else to do. Do you know that Becca . . . that is . . ."

"I know that Becca is Mattie's daughter. Mattie and I are close friends."

"Just friends?"

"Yes."

"Interesting," Maria said. "Anyway, Slade, Becca must never know who her real mother is."

"I understand that. She won't hear it from me."

"Slade, my Becca—I love her as though she were my own—has been through so much these past weeks. Jed's dying was a shock to us all, but Becca is taking it so hard. She was very close to her pa, and he thought the sun rose and set because she wished it. Jed was hardly a month in his grave when Henry Folger came courting Becca. Folger, that swine, wants the Bonnie Blue, and he'll do anything to get it. I'm glad you're here. Becca needs you. We all do."

"I have to convince *her* of that. She definitely has a mind of her own."

"She's feisty, that's for sure, and brave, and . . . well, she's Becca. She won't give up the Bonnie Blue without a hard fight, Slade, and I'm frightened for her." She paused and glanced toward the door. "You best get to the dining room. You and I will talk again later. I do praise the Lord that you're here. I knew Mattie would know what to do. You just stand your ground and tell Becca you're staying. Oh, mercy, she's liable to throw a fit of temper."

Slade chuckled. "Wouldn't surprise me at all. I'll speak with you again when I can."

As Slade left the kitchen, Maria clasped her hands together and looked heavenward for a long moment, then returned to the stove nodding decisively.

Three

In her room, Becca washed her face and hands in the large china bowl on her dresser, then undid the black ribbon that held her hair back. The heavy, auburn tresses fell in waves halfway down her back. She brushed her hair and retied the ribbon, then glanced at her reflection in the oval mirror above the dresser. Her eyes revealed a familiar, lingering sadness, as she'd known they would, along with fatigue.

She braced her hands on the dresser and leaned closer, peering at her image. There was something else there in her eyes, she realized, a flicker of brightness, and her cheeks had a rosy glow.

The memory of Slade standing by the pump without his shirt flitted through her mind, and she frowned as she felt again the funny flutter along her spine, as well as a strange heat that pulsed within her.

She was acting like a child who'd never seen a handsome man before, she admonished herself. She'd grown up surrounded by men on the Bonnie Blue, and had always been comfortable around them. She enjoyed their company, and had spent many pleasant afternoons and evenings with young men from neighboring ranches. No, men were not strangers to her.

Yet . . .

She turned from the mirror and smoothed her dress over her hips. Yes, she admitted to herself, Slade Ironbow was very different from any other man she'd ever met.

Power and strength emanated from him, and a nearly tangible essence of virility and masculinity. Good-looking? Yes. Well-built? Yes. Dangerous? Very.

He had an incredible voice, she mused. And eyes. They were as dark as coal, and had seemed to look right through her dress to her heated skin. Who was he, this man who evoked such new and strange sensations within her? What was he doing on the Bonnie Blue?

Well, she intended to find out exactly who he was and why he was there. She would eat supper with the mysterious Mr. Ironbow, and if his answers left any niggling doubts in her mind that he might be working for Henry Folger, she'd send Slade Ironbow packing.

Becca squared her shoulders, lifted her chin, and left the bedroom. As she neared the dining room, she told herself the fluttering butterflies in her stomach and the trembling in her knees were solely because of hunger.

When Slade had entered the dining room and discovered Becca was not yet there, he'd wandered down the hall to the large living room. Glancing around, he was struck immediately by the welcoming atmosphere of the room.

Richly decorated with massive dark wood furniture and earth colors, with a huge stone fireplace covering nearly one entire wall, the room spoke of the rugged West, of Texas, and a man who had taken great pride in what he possessed. While the decor had a definite masculine flair, Slade had no difficulty picturing Becca Colten in the room.

He'd seen her passion as fury when she'd faced him and the men from Four Aces. What if that passion turned to desire? What if it were directed at him, and he took her into his arms and loved her? It would be, he knew, a magnificent joining, unlike anything he'd experienced before.

"Mr. Ironbow," Becca said from the doorway, "you weren't in the dining room. Maria is putting supper on now, if you'd care to join me."

He turned to face her. "Slade."

She inclined her head. "Slade. Shall we go?" She turned with a swish of dark skirt and disappeared.

Slade chuckled as he followed her from the room. "Snooty again."

A glittering chandelier ablaze with candles lighted the dining room. Becca seated herself at the end of a gleaming cherry-wood table that was at least ten feet long. She sat, Slade surmised, in the chair that had been her father's, making it clear *she* was now owner of the Bonnie Blue.

Maria was putting platters of food on the table—roast beef, potatoes, beans, and biscuits. Another place was set directly to Becca's right. Slade crossed the room to his chair. Becca didn't look at him.

"Would you consider removing your gun while we eat?" she asked.

"No," he said, sitting down.

Maria laughed. "You asked, you got an answer, Becca. Now then, you two dig right in there. And you see that you eat plenty, Becca Colten. You're wasting away to nothing more than a little bird." With that, Maria bustled out of the room.

A fragile little bird, Slade thought, easily frightened and hurt. Well, not while he was there.

"Help yourself," Becca said, lifting a slice of roast beef onto her plate.

He wanted her, Slade thought suddenly. He wanted to touch her cheek to see if her skin was as soft as it appeared. He wanted to pull the ribbon from her hair and weave his fingers through the heavy, silken locks, watch them float over her breasts, her bare breasts. He wanted to nestle her to him, kiss her tempting lips, then lower her to a bed . . .

As Slade's body tightened from his unexpected wayward thoughts, he cleared his throat roughly and filled his plate with the steaming food. They ate in silence for several minutes.

He had very refined table manners, Becca thought, watching Slade from beneath her lashes. He was no stranger to dining at elegant tables. Women probably often invited him to join them for a meal. And to join them in bed? Probably.

Becca stiffened. Shame on you, she scolded herself. She'd never before entertained such wanton thoughts concerning a man and a bed. Never.

It was one thing to stand on her front porch, rifle in hand, and square off against the formidable Mr. Ironbow. It was quite another to be alone with him in the somewhat intimate atmosphere of two people sharing supper. Shouldn't Maria be hovering around, acting as a chaperone of sorts?

Becca took a sip of coffee and told herself to calm down. There was, after all, a definite purpose to her having supper with Slade. It was vitally important that she learn why he had suddenly arrived at the Bonnie Blue.

But how could she even think when he was somehow filling the room to overflowing with his vibrant, masculine presence? He was just so male, and just so there, and she didn't seem able to draw enough air into her lungs.

"Mr. . . . Slade, suppose we get down to business," she said, hoping her voice was steady. "Why are you here? And, please, don't say that you're my new foreman."

"I *am* your new foreman," he said.

"No, you are not," she said stiffly. "I don't even know who you are, how you happened to appear on my land. I'm not convinced you're not working for Folger."

"Never met the man." Slade finished his potatoes and piled more on his plate.

"You just happened by accidentally?"

"No."

"Damn it," she exclaimed, "would you give me some straight answers?"

"Swearing like a drunken cowboy again. Ladies aren't supposed to swear, Miss Colten."

"I'm warning you, Slade Ironbow, I've had enough of this. You tell me what I want to know, or saddle up and ride out of here."

Slade took a deep swallow of coffee, carefully replaced the china cup in the saucer, then looked directly at her.

"I'm here," he said quietly, "because you're in trouble, and you need me to be here. I'm going to be your foreman because it's the best way to handle this."

"But I don't even know you. Why would I or the Bonnie Blue matter to you?"

"Let's just say I owe a debt to your father."

"My father? You knew him?"

"Not directly. He did a kind thing for someone I know who can't repay the favor. *I* can. I intend to."

"I'm to understand that you're acting on someone else's behalf? Repaying an act of kindness my father showed this other person?"

"Close enough."

"Why?" she asked, leaning toward him. "Why would you do that?"

He shrugged. "The person asked me to."

"You'd walk into a potentially dangerous situation involving people you don't even know because someone asked you to?"

"Yes."

Becca sat back in her chair and stared at him. "That's crazy."

"No." He took a bite of potatoes.

"Henry Folger is determined to get this ranch. You could be hurt, even killed, repaying a debt that isn't yours."

"I wasn't planning on getting myself killed."

She pounded her fist once on the table in frustration. "You may not have any say in the matter!"

"I generally have an opinion about living or dying, Miss Colten. So far, I've picked living. How many men do you have working for you?"

"Thirty-five, give or take a few."

"Do you know them all? Trust them?"

"I know most of them, and they've sworn their loyalty to me. Ten, maybe a dozen, are drifters who haven't been here very long."

"How did your foreman break his leg?"

"His horse threw him. Just—just the way my father's did. My pa was an excellent rider, and was on his own mount when it happened. The same holds true for Frank, the foreman. I find it hard to believe . . ." Her voice trailed off.

"That they were accidents? Miss Colten . . . Becca, do you think your father was purposely killed? Murdered by Henry Folger?"

"Yes," she whispered, fighting back sudden tears. "Yes, I do. I also think Frank was gotten out of the way deliberately too." She shook her head violently. "But how? No shots were heard to spook those horses. They were fine, then the next moment they went down. My father . . . my father struck his head on a rock and died instantly.

Frank's leg was broken three days ago. He's in the bunkhouse with wooden splints on his leg, and he's in terrible pain. He said he can't figure out what happened. His horse just seemed to crumble beneath him, and he was thrown. He—Why am I telling you all this?"

"I have to know. I have to have a clear picture of things. Who's acting as foreman now?"

"Yancey Perkins. He's been here for years. He's worried, though; says he's too old to handle the job. There have been other incidents, too, in the past month. A mile of fence was cut, one of the steam-operated pumps we were using to irrigate a far section that had gone dry was destroyed, a natural water hole was polluted. All the men are getting nervous, wondering what Folger is going to do next."

Slade nodded. "Nervous men make mistakes. In the morning you can introduce me as the new foreman, and I'll take it from there."

"You certainly will not," she said, sitting bolt upright.

"Yes, I will."

"This is my ranch, Mr. Ironbow."

He sighed. "I don't doubt that you'll remind me of that every two minutes . . . ma'am. All right, I'll report in to you, tell you everything that I'm doing, what I see, what I think. That suit you?"

"I never agreed to your being the foreman."

"Do you have a better idea?"

"How do I know I can trust you?" she asked, leaning toward him again. "Answer that one. Just how in heaven's name do I know that I can trust you?"

"Becca," he said, looking directly into her eyes, "you can trust me."

Becca met his gaze, her heart racing. Slade's voice had seemed to drop an octave, and she was pinned in place by the fathomless depths of his dark eyes. The sound of her own name floated over her like soft velvet, 'warming and caressing her, comforting her, quieting her fears.

Yes, she thought, she could trust Slade Ironbow.

"All right," she said, tearing her gaze from his. "We'll try it. I'll be riding with you, of course."

"What?"

"This is a working ranch. Therefore, I work. I rode the range with my father from the time I was ten years old."

"You don't belong out there," Slade said, frowning.

"Oh? I suppose you feel that because I'm a woman I should sit around fluttering my eyelashes in between having babies."

"You've got something against babies?" he asked gruffly.

"Of course not, but since I don't have a husband, babies are not on my mind at the moment. I saddle up at dawn like everyone else."

Slade sat back in his chair and glared at her. "From the sound of things, I'm going to have my hands full around here as it is. I won't have time to look after you."

"No one looks after me, Slade Ironbow. I'm perfectly capable of taking care of myself. My father knew it, the men know it, and I suggest you believe it."

"When I see it," he said, his eyes narrowing, "then I'll believe it."

"Fine. If you're finished eating I'll take you to the bunkhouse. Introductions can be made tonight, and I'm sure there's a spare bed out there."

"No."

"I beg your pardon?"

"I'm staying here in the house."

Becca jumped to her feet. "You certainly are not!"

Slade stood slowly, his jaw set in a hard line as he towered over her. She stared up at him, wide-eyed.

"I'm here," he said, his voice ominously low, "not only to protect the Bonnie Blue, but you as well. That will be made clear to the men, so your lily-white reputation won't be damaged. If you insist on going out on the range, you're never to be out of my sight. In addition, you don't go into town, or off to visit with your lady friends, nothing, unless you clear it with me first. And if you ever take on riders from Four Aces all alone like you did today, I'll personally wring your pretty little neck."

She planted her hands on her hips, gulping air into her lungs before she attempted to speak.

"Slade Ironbow," she said, her voice trembling with rage, "you are—"

"Right," Maria interrupted, hurrying into the room. "Mercy me, it's so good to know you're going to be safe from harm, Becca, until this trouble with Folger is settled."

"Maria!" Becca exclaimed. "How can you take sides with this arrogant, rude man?"

"Because I love you, Becca," Maria said softly, "and because your pa loved you. Jed Colten would like knowing someone's watching over you. Now, you swallow your temper and your stubborn streak, and use the common sense the good Lord gave you. You need Slade, we all do, and you'd best get used to following his orders until Henry Folger has been stopped. Are you listening to me, Becca Colten?"

Becca glared at Maria, then Slade, then Maria again. "Yes, I'm listening," she said tightly. "We'll do this your way . . . for now, Mr. Ironbow," she added, glowering at him again. "I'll cooperate . . . for now. But I sure as hell don't have to like it." She whirled and stomped out of the room.

"Swearing again," Slade said, shaking his head. "She does have a temper."

Maria laughed. "That she does, but she said she'll cooperate, and she will. She won't smile about it, but she'll do it."

"I want the room next to hers."

"I'll make up the bed with fresh linens. Thank you, Slade, for coming. I'll rest easier tonight knowing you're here."

"Maria, do you think Jed Colten was murdered?"

"Yes, I do. Frank breaking his leg was no accident, either, in my opinion. I don't know why those horses went down, but . . ." She shook her head. "There's no proof, though."

"The town near here, Jubele, what about its sheriff? Is there any chance that he answers to Folger?"

"Brady Webster? Mercy, no. Brady's as honest as the day is long. He told me himself that Jed Colten's being thrown from his horse didn't make any sense. Brady was mighty upset when Frank was hurt the same way. But he says there's no proof of any wrongdoing."

Slade nodded.

"Well, I'll go make up your bed, Slade. I'll look in on Becca, too, and make sure she isn't still angry as a wet hen."

"She's quite a woman," Slade said, staring at the doorway Becca had disappeared through.

Maria looked at Slade, a smile curving her lips. Her smiled broadened as he continued to gaze at the doorway. When she turned to leave the room, she was humming a happy tune.

Four

Mattie slipped out of the back door of the Silver Spur and strolled across the grassy rear area. The bright moon acted like a silvery beacon to light her way, although she could have reached her destination with no difficulty on the darkest of nights.

The Silver Spur was busy but under control, the mid-week crowd low-key and relaxed. Abe knew where she went when she wanted some fresh air and a few quiet minutes, and would send someone for her if the need arose.

Mattie smiled as she saw her white swing gleaming in the moonlight, suspended by chains from the branch of a sturdy tree. Oh, how she adored her swing.

She arranged her royal-blue silk skirt around her as she sat down on the white bench. Leaning back, she set the swing in motion, then closed her eyes and took a deep breath of the spring night air.

She'd woven such fantasies on this swing, she mused.

In the five years since she'd had this private place to escape to, she'd imagined glorious things for herself, and almost all depicted her as a fine, well-bred woman. She was respected and loved, surrounded by her children and a man who cherished her.

Such hopeless dreams, Mattie thought, opening her eyes. And this night she would not be allowed the luxury of escape, for her thoughts were centered on Slade, Becca, and the Bonnie Blue. What had Slade found when he arrived at the ranch in Texas? Were Becca and Maria and Slade in great danger?

Becca and Slade. Sitting there on her swing in the peaceful glow of moonlight, Mattie would weave a splendid fantasy for them.

Becca, a bride, her shimmering gown made of yards and yards of white satin and lace, with hundreds of delicate seed pearls decorating the bodice. A gossamer veil would hide her face as she walked down the aisle to meet the man who loved her, the man she would find happiness with for all her days. Slade Ironbow.

And Slade, the groom, would be resplendent in a black suit that emphasized the night darkness of his hair and eyes, the glow of his bronzed skin. His eyes would be warm, reflecting the love in his heart for the woman who was to become his wife.

Mattie sighed. Such foolishness she was creating. Slade Ironbow would never love one woman, stay in one place. He saw himself as a creature of the wind. And Becca? Mattie really didn't know her own daughter, didn't know if she was pampered and spoiled, the product of a wealthy man who'd given his child everything she'd demanded.

And there sat Mattie Muldoon, she thought ruefully, fantasizing that Becca and Slade were perfectly suited for each other, would fall madly in love and marry with hearts bursting with joy.

Enough, she told herself. She was being silly, wanting

for Becca what she herself had always yearned for and could never have.

She sighed again and shook her head.

"That's a sad, sad sound," a voice said.

She gasped and stiffened on the swing. The moonlight clearly identified the man who stepped out of the shadows of the trees.

"Doc! You scared me. Whatever are you doing back here?"

"Looking for you." He walked over to her. "When you weren't inside, I knew there was a good chance you'd be out here on your swing."

She smiled up at him. "I didn't realize anyone knew I escaped to this spot except Abe."

"I've seen you here many times. I just stayed in the shadows, allowed you your privacy, but made sure no one bothered you. It could be dangerous out here alone with drunken cowboys on the loose." He smiled. "You always seem so content on your swing, Mattie, as though you're painting pretty pictures in your mind."

"Oh, dear, you've caught me," she said with a soft laugh. "That's exactly what I do. This is the one place where I can forget my responsibilities, everything that needs my attention and supervision, and just daydream." She pulled her skirts in and moved to one side. "Would you care to join me, Doc?"

"I'd be honored, ma'am," he said, bowing, then settled next to her on the swing. "You know, everything runs so smoothly at the Silver Spur that I doubt many people realize what an intelligent, organized businesswoman you are, Mattie. I respect that. Lord knows my record books are a scribbled mess. I've turned them over to my assistant to handle, along with the task of keeping track of what supplies we need."

"I like to be aware of everything that's going on at the Spur. I wouldn't be comfortable having anyone else doing my books or ordering goods. When I need a break from it all, I come sit on my swing."

"And a fine swing it is."

"I was so excited the day Abe hung it for me. I guess there's still a touch of a little girl hiding inside me. I sit out here and paint big beautiful pictures in my mind."

"There's nothing wrong with having dreams," Doc said. "But tonight your sigh sounded sad." He slipped one arm behind her on the top of the swing, careful not to touch her.

"Oh, sometimes I . . . Never mind. It's too beautiful a night for gloomy thoughts. Look at that sky, Doc. It's a silvery glow. Just beautiful." Her gaze swept the heavens.

Doc's eyes were riveted on her. "Just beautiful," he repeated.

Mattie glanced down at her silk skirt, smoothing wrinkles that weren't there. "I suppose I'd best get back inside."

"Not yet. I'd like to talk to you."

"Oh?" she said, still not looking at him.

"Slade's been gone for several days, but it's taken me this long to get up the courage to come here, Mattie. There are things that I want, need, to say, and I've been over it all a hundred times in my mind since Slade left. I finally decided just to speak the words, even if I do it poorly."

"Doc . . ."

"Now, just listen, Mattie Muldoon. First off, I know that you and Slade are not . . . That is, everyone thinks that the two of you are . . . Dammit, Mattie, I know you and Slade aren't lovers!"

Her head snapped up and she stared at Doc with wide eyes. "What?"

"Slade told me the truth the night before he left."

She jumped to her feet. "What!"

Doc took her hand and tugged gently. "Sit back down here."

"Slade told you that he and I . . . I swear I'll strangle that man!"

Doc laughed. "He figured as much and told me not to say anything until he was way clear of Dodge. It took me far longer than that to get up the courage, though." He tugged again on her hand. "Mattie, please, sit back down here. Please?"

She plopped back down on the swing, her eyes still wide as she stared at him. "Slade told you the truth about us? He told you that we're only friends? Slade?"

"Surprised me, too, believe me. I've never heard Slade say so much in one sitting. He said it needed saying, even though he knew you'd be ready to shoot him on sight."

"Needed saying?" Mattie repeated, nearly shouting. "Slade Ironbow has gone loco."

"No, Slade Ironbow knows that I . . ." Doc tightened his grip on her hand. "I am deeply in love with you, Mattie Muldoon. He wanted to tell me that he wasn't standing in my way. And so, here I am, hat in hand, heart on my sleeve, telling you that I do, indeed, love you very much."

Mattie shook her head so sharply, a lock of hair escaped her chignon. "Don't say that. Doc, I'm going back inside, and we'll forget that this conversation ever took place. Just don't speak another word on the subject. Is that clear?"

"Why? Because you care nothing for me? You don't want to hurt my feelings? Why can't I say that I love you with all my heart, Mattie? I truly do, you know, and have for a long time."

"No, no," she said, shaking her head again. "You can't, and I won't hear another word of this."

"Yes, you will. I love you, and I plan to come courting. You see, Mattie, I have every intention of asking you to be my wife. I want to marry you, and have a child with you, God willing."

Pulling her hand free, Mattie leaped to her feet so quickly, the swing swayed wildly for a moment. Doc simply smiled at her.

"You're the one who's loco," she declared, then narrowed her eyes. "Have you been drinking?"

"Not a drop."

She planted her hands on her hips. "I won't listen to this for another minute. This isn't kind, Doctor Willis. Not kind at all. If this is your idea of a joke, I find no humor in it."

He rose to stand in front of her. "It's the truth. I love you."

"You can't! Doc, I'm Mattie Muldoon, the owner of the Silver Spur saloon. Remember?"

"Best saloon in Dodge City."

"I made my living early on as one of the girls, Doc, and you know that."

"That was a long time ago. We all have things in our past best forgotten."

"Forgotten?" she repeated, her voice rising. "No one has forgotten, including me. Besides, everyone believes I've been Slade's woman all these years."

"But I know differently, and I'm the one who's in love with you."

"You are not in love with me!"

He took a step closer to her and cradled her face in his hands. "Oh, but I am."

Run! Mattie's mind screamed. He was going to kiss her, she could tell, and she mustn't allow this to happen. But how many nights had she sat on her swing, dreaming of Doc Willis kissing her, holding her . . . No! Run!

"I'm going to kiss you now, Mattie," he said huskily.

No! "Yes," she whispered. "No, no, I—"

He lowered his head and claimed her mouth in a kiss

so soft, so sweet, that tears sprang to Mattie's eyes. Her knees trembled, and she clutched his shoulders for support. The kiss intensified as he dropped his hands to her back and pulled her to him, crushing her breasts against his chest.

Oh, yes, Mattie thought dreamily. She'd waited for this, imagined this. Doc was there, at last. He was kissing her, holding her, igniting within her a desire she'd thought long dead.

He slowly lifted his head, but didn't release her as he gazed into her eyes. "I love you, Mattie. I want to marry you and spend the rest of my life with you. Maybe you'll never come to love me as I love you, but if you care for me even a little, I'll count myself the luckiest man. It'll be the happiest, proudest day of my life when you become my wife."

Mattie fell from her hazy fantasies with a painful thud. "Proud? Oh, Doc, you're insane. I was a whore. I run a house of pleasure. There's nothing about me to make any man proud. I'm alone, I always will be, and I take care of myself. You'd be proud to have me as your wife? You have truly lost all sense. I accepted my life as it is years ago. You best accept it, too, and stop this foolishness this very instant."

Doc gently gripped her shoulders and gave her a small shake. "I won't hear another word of your saying I shouldn't be proud to call you my wife. I'm coming courting, Miss Muldoon. Get used to that idea, because the whole town is going to know quite well what I'm doing."

"Oh, dear Lord," she whispered. "Doc, would you think clearly for one second? Everyone in Dodge believes that Slade and I . . . They'll be waiting for Slade to come back and call you out and . . ."

"These folks will just have to live with the disappointment that Slade Ironbow isn't going to shoot me dead," Doc said dryly.

"Well, I'm going to shoot *him* dead!" she exclaimed. "This is so wrong. You're a respectable citizen of Dodge City and I'm a—"

"Don't say it," Doc warned her. "You're speaking of the woman I love and intend to marry." He paused and smiled at her. "I'll bid you good night now, Miss Muldoon."

"But—"

He pulled her close and gave her a hard, fast kiss. She staggered when he released her.

"Good night, ma'am," he said formally. "It has indeed been a pleasure speaking with you, and sharing your swing. Oh, and my name is Jim. From here on out, you'll call me Jim." He strode past her and left.

She spun around and watched him go. "But, Doc . . ."

"Jim," he repeated over his shoulder. "I'll come calling tomorrow, Miss Muldoon."

As he disappeared into the darkness, Mattie sank onto the swing and stared after him. Her fingertips came to rest on her lips, and she relived the feel and taste of Doc's mouth on hers.

"I never knew his name was Jim," she whispered.

At noon the next day, Dr. James Willis entered the general store owned and operated by the Widow Sullivan. While there were two other general stores in Dodge, one larger and better stocked than this one, Doc had made his choice carefully. This store had exactly what he needed—Widow Sullivan, and her reputation for being the busiest gossip in all of Dodge City. If you did it, Widow Sullivan knew about it. And she had perfected her ability to spread any news, large or small, interesting or dull, as fast as a greased pig.

"Good day, Widow Sullivan," Doc said as he strode into the store, touching his fingertips to the brim of his hat.

He walked directly to the counter and delivered his very best smile to the tall, broad woman standing behind it.

"Howdy do, Doc," the widow said in her booming voice. "What can I do for you today?"

Doc sighed dramatically. "I find myself in a great dilemma, ma'am."

"Is that a fact?" Widow Sullivan asked, leaning toward him, eyes sparkling with anticipation. "Well, why don't you just tell me all your troubles. It's truly amazing how much help can come from an extra mind working on a problem."

"Well, you see, I'm going courting and—"

Widow Sullivan clasped her hands together in delight. "You're going courting? Land's sake, this is marvelous, just marvelous. It's time you had yourself a wife, Doc Willis, if I do say so myself."

"My sentiments exactly," he said, nodding. "My problem is I don't know where to start. I'm going calling today, and feel I should take a small token to my lady. But"—he threw up his hands in despair—"I have no idea what would be proper."

"I have the perfect thing," Widow Sullivan gushed. "Came from back East. Chocolates in a pretty box. Most highfalutin thing I ever saw."

"Are you sure it's proper to take chocolates to a lady the first time I go calling?"

"Mercy, yes. And you say, 'Sweets for the sweet.' "

Doc groaned silently. "Yes, ma'am, I'll surely remember to say that."

"Wonderful." The widow removed a small, gold-foil box from a shelf behind the counter and placed it in front of Doc. "That's fifty cents."

Doc paid her and picked up the box. "Thank you for all your help. You're really most kind." He turned to leave. "Good day."

"Oh, Doc?" the widow called, smiling brightly.

He looked back at her. "Yes?"

"I'm just a lonely widow, you know, and the news of love simply warms my heart. It would bring such sunshine into my life if you'd share the name of the dear woman you're courting."

Doc opened his mouth to answer just as the door opened and two women, Emma Virginia Tappitt and her daughter, entered the store. He slid them a quick look, then raised his voice when he spoke.

"It would brighten your day to know who I'm courting, Widow Sullivan?" he asked. "Who I'm going calling on to give these chocolates to?"

"Oh, my, yes," Widow Sullivan said.

Emma Virginia and her daughter inched closer.

"I see no harm in telling you who it is," Doc said, "since my intentions are strictly honorable. I intend to make her my wife, if she'll have me. I have to convince her that I'm good husband material."

"Nonsense," Emma Virginia said. "You're the best catch in town, Doc Willis. Unless she's a silly fool, she'll know that."

"Doc was speaking to me, Emma Virginia," Widow Sullivan said huffily. "Go on, Doc."

"Yes," he said. "The object of my affections, my bright star, my one and only is . . ."

"Yes, yes?" Widow Sullivan said.

"Miss Mattie Muldoon." He beamed. "Good day to you, ladies."

With that, Dr. Jim Willis went out of the store, leaving three shocked women staring after him with their mouths open and their eyes wide.

Doc strode along the wooden sidewalk, nodding at men and smiling and touching the brim of his hat as he passed women. The box of chocolates was tucked securely under his arm.

When he reached the Silver Spur, he saw that the

double doors behind the louvered half-doors were closed. He knocked briskly, and a minute later Abe opened one of the doors.

"Howdy, Doc," he said. "Thought you knew we don't open until the middle of the afternoon."

"I've come to see Mattie."

"Oh, well, that's fine, I guess. They're all just sitting here drinking coffee. If you don't mind seeing a bunch of women in their dressing gowns and no paint on their faces, come on in."

"Thank you, Abe."

Doc squared his shoulders and entered the saloon. Mattie and her girls were sitting around two tables. It was odd to see the Spur empty of men, and the girls looking no different from Dodge's most respected matrons, first thing in the morning. Mattie sat up straight when she saw him, and all of the women turned to stare at him.

"Good day, ladies," he said.

"Doc," Mattie whispered, rising slowly. She was wearing a green silk dressing gown and her hair was loose, tumbling in waves past her shoulders.

"Jim," he said, striding confidently toward her. "You're to call me Jim, remember?" He extended the box of chocolates to her, and she took it into her shaking hands. "These are for you. I have officially begun my courting of you, Miss Muldoon, just as I said I would." He leaned down and brushed his lips over hers. "Widow Sullivan said I was to say 'Sweets for the sweet' when I gave you the chocolates. So, consider it said."

"Widow Sullivan knows that . . ." Mattie gasped. "Oh, Doc, what have you done?"

"Started courting you, ma'am." He smiled and tipped his hat, then spun on his heel and left the saloon.

Mattie stared at the door, the box of chocolates, then the door again. "Oh, dear Lord."

Abe shook his head. "There's trouble ahead, there's bad trouble ahead. When Slade Ironbow hears of this . . . Oh, there is trouble ahead."

"Abe, hush," Mattie said, sinking back onto her chair.

Ellen, one of the girls, sighed dreamily. "A real gentleman comin' a courtin'. That is just the finest thing I ever did see."

"You best see it real fast," Abe said. "Doc Willis will be in his grave when Slade gets back."

"Stop it, Abe," Mattie said, running a fingertip over the gold-foil box.

"You know Slade's going to shoot Doc dead," Abe said. "Too bad. I like Doc. Him and Slade is friends too. Slade will have to shoot him, though. Call him out, of course, to keep it legal."

"Maybe Slade won't hear tell of this," Belle said.

"Didn't you listen to Doc?" Abe asked. "The Widow Sullivan knows."

"Oh." Belle shrugged. "That settles that. All of Dodge City knows."

"Yep," Abe said. "I'm going to miss Doc. Thought he had more brains than this. He just signed his own death papers."

"Abraham, that is enough," Mattie said sternly. "This is the first box of chocolates I've ever received in my life; now don't you go and ruin it for me. I will, somehow, get Doc Willis to stop this nonsense of his, but at the moment I'd like to enjoy my chocolates."

Abe grinned. "Yes, ma'am. Must admit that's a right fancy box he brought you."

"Could you open it?" Ellen asked. "We wouldn't dream of askin' you for none, but I never saw chocolates before. Did Doc say his name was Jim?"

"Yes," Mattie said, carefully lifting the cover of the box. "Jim."

"Fancy that," Belle said. "I thought his name was Doc.

Oh, look! Oh, Mattie, aren't they beautiful? So that's chocolates. See how they're sittin' in a paper basket, each and every one? Amazing. They smell funny, but they sure are pretty."

All the girls gathered around Mattie, peering into the box and oohing and aahing over the treasure.

Mattie blinked back her tears as she stared at the chocolates. Oh, Jim, she thought dismally. Dumb, darling Jim. What a fool thing to have gone and done. The news that Doc Willis was courting Mattie Muldoon would be all over Dodge by nightfall, thanks to Widow Sullivan. Doc had stirred up a hornet's nest, and Mattie had no idea how to quiet it. He would be hurt by his actions, his reputation soiled by his courting her. She'd told Abe she'd stop Doc somehow, but what if it was too late, the damage already done?

"Well," she said, forcing a lightness to her voice, "I must be getting upstairs." She put the lid back on the chocolates and stood up. "I have to work on the books." Carrying the golden box, she hurried across the room and up the stairs.

"Was she crying?" Bella asked, frowning.

"I would be if someone came courtin' and brought me chocolates," Ellen said. "Sure never goin' to happen to me. Imagine a real gentleman comin' courtin'."

"A dead gentleman," Abe said.

"Abe," Belle said, "shut up."

"Maybe Slade is ready for a change of women," Clara said, fluffing her hair. "He does take a fancy to me at times, you know."

"Clara," Belle said, "shut up." Clara slouched back in her chair and pouted. "Those chocolates sure were pretty," Belle went on, "but didn't you think they smelled funny?"

"Belle," two women said in unison, "shut up."

•   •   •

Upstairs, Mattie restlessly paced her sitting room, her gaze continually drawn to the shiny, gold-foil box of chocolates sitting on one of the tables. She hadn't slept well the night before, and had awakened feeling as tired as when she'd gone to bed. Now, her head was pounding as she replayed in her mind the scene with Doc downstairs. How could he have done such a fool thing, bought chocolates from Widow Sullivan, then marched right up to the Spur in broad daylight?

Mattie walked into the bedroom and brushed back the curtain over the window. Below, her swing gleamed in the sun and swayed slightly in the breeze. Memories of the previous night rushed over her—memories of being held in Jim's arms, being kissed by him, hearing him say that he loved her and wanted her to be his wife. A magical night, best forgotten. A night she knew she would never forget.

A now-familiar ache tightened her throat, and she had neither the strength nor the desire to stop the tears that filled her eyes. She was going to cry. She was going to cry because she was tired, her head hurt, and she was worried about Becca, and Slade, and Doc. She was going to cry because at the moment she didn't know how to solve her problems. She was going to cry because she was alone and lonely.

And when she was finished crying, she decided, as the tears started to fall, she would figure out what she was going to do.

"Hey, Doc. Can I talk to you for a minute?"

Doc looked up from his desk at the small man standing in his office doorway. Dressed in a black suit, the man was nervously twirling his hat in his hands.

"Howdy, Harvey," Doc said. "How's the funeral business?"

"Fair."

"What can I do for you? I really don't have any bodies lying around here waiting for your services."

"No, no, of course you don't. I . . . um . . . Well, Doc, a man needs to be looking ahead in his life, making plans for . . . things."

"Things?" Doc repeated, raising his eyebrows.

"Yes. You see, if you pay in advance for your coffin and burial, you don't add financial burden to your grieving kin. Yes, sir, a man needs to look ahead. I've got a special price for you, Doc, that you can't afford to pass up. Think of the peace of mind it will give you to know this is all tended to."

"I'm not planning on dying in the near future, Harvey," Doc said pleasantly, "but thanks for dropping by and making me an offer."

"You're not being considerate of your kin," Harvey said. "They'll be stuck with your burial costs when Mr. Iron-bow—that is . . . Well, I'll be seeing you, Doc." He spun around and started back through the door.

"Hold it!"

Harvey stopped and turned tentatively to face him again. "Yes?"

"Are you saying you came here to give me a cut rate for my funeral now, because you figure I'll be dead once Slade Ironbow gets back here?"

"Oh, well, I . . ."

"Harvey?"

"Hell's fire, Doc, the word is out that you're courting Mattie Muldoon. Now I'm not one to pass judgment. By the time I deal with folks, they're in no position to be expressing their opinion on anything. But facts are facts, Doc, and as a businessman I have to be practical. It would be a kindness to your kin to pay for your funeral now, because everyone knows your days are numbered.

Slade Ironbow is going to shoot you into tomorrow when he finds out you been courting Mattie Muldoon."

Dr. James Willis put his head back and roared with laughter. Harvey inched his way out the door, his eyes wide with shock. He told the next six people he saw that Doc Willis was not in his right mind.

When Doc's assistant entered the office twenty minutes later, he found his mentor trying to cure himself of a painful case of the hiccups.

Five

Slade was up before dawn. As he strode to the kitchen, he knew that the scowl he'd seen on his face while he'd shaved was still firmly in place. He had not slept well, tossing and turning throughout the night, his bed linens ending up on the floor in a tangled heap.

Always before he'd slept when he commanded his body to do so. He'd perfected the knack of grabbing quick naps and awakening refreshed. When he slept, he did so lightly, a section of his mind alert for any hint of danger. But not last night. He couldn't remember ever being so consumed by thoughts that he'd been unable to relax and sleep.

Consumed by thoughts of Becca Colten.

Hearing her moving around in the room next to his, he'd been able to see her in his mind's eye so clearly, she might as well have been in *his* room. He'd remembered how anger had flashed in her eyes; how her prim, high-necked mourning dress had molded to her full breasts and her waist, so tiny he was sure he could circle it with his hands. He'd pictured her brushing her hair until it shone like an auburn waterfall tumbling down her back.

Oh, yes, he thought dryly, stopping outside the kitchen door, he'd spent a very long, uncomfortable night, thanks to Miss Colten. His wandering mind had lingered on the tantalizing shape of her lips, and he'd envisioned himself taking Becca into his arms and covering her mouth with his. His body had grown hard, aching with desire, as he'd imagined lowering her to the bed and meshing his body with hers.

Nothing like this had ever happened to him before!

"Damn," he muttered, then pushed open the door and strode heavily into the kitchen.

Maria was standing in front of the stove, and glanced up when she heard him. " 'Morning, Slade. Coffee is ready and the eggs will be along in a few minutes. Sun's coming up. Shouldn't be too hot out on the range this time of year. Another month, though, and we'll be feeling the heat."

Slade poured coffee into a mug, then sat at the wooden table.

"Hope you don't mind eating breakfast in the kitchen," Maria went on. "Becca and Jed always took their breakfast out here."

"Fine," he said.

He took off his Stetson and set it on the chair next to him. So, where was Miss Colten? he wondered. Still in bed, probably. She'd no doubt slept like a baby and would get up when she was good and ready. For all her talk about riding with him, he was sure it was at her leisure, whenever the mood struck. She'd be in no hurry to leave the comforts of her fancy house with Maria waiting on her hand and foot.

The back door opened and Becca strode in. "Slade," she said coolly, nodding at him as she headed for the coffeepot on the stove.

Slade's gaze skimmed over her body. She was clad in dark denim pants that emphasized the slimness of her hips and length of her legs. She wore boots and a white cotton shirt, and her hair was plaited into a single braid that hung down her back.

She poured her coffee and started toward the table. He watched her with heavy-lidded eyes, unable to look away from her breasts, barely discernible beneath the shirt. When she sat down opposite him, his gaze lifted to the lips that had helped create his unsettled night. He felt his body tighten, and his anger increased.

"I was out to the bunkhouse," she said, not looking at him. "I wanted to make sure the men didn't leave until they'd met you. I told them your name, said you were the new foreman until Frank's leg is healed, and that you were also my bodyguard of sorts, which was why you were staying in the house."

She paused and sipped her coffee. When Slade didn't comment, she continued.

"Some of the men have heard of you. They were buzzing among themselves when I left. They'll wait until you speak to them before they head out to start their chores."

"Hot food," Maria said, bustling across the large room with two plates. "Eggs, bacon, hash browns. Now, you dig in and clean those plates, both of you."

"Thank you," Becca said, smiling at her.

"Thanks," Slade said gruffly.

"Do you always wake up this cheerfully, Mr. Ironbow," Becca asked sweetly, "or is this a special treat for the Bonnie Blue?"

"Becca," Maria said warningly as she returned to the stove, "mind your manners."

Slade scooped up some eggs, then glanced at Becca. "Do you always go around dressed like a man?"

She stiffened. "I beg your pardon?"

"You heard me," he said, munching on a crisp slice of bacon.

"These are my working clothes, Mr. Ironbow, and are quite appropriate for a working ranch."

"And appropriate for wiggling your cute little behind in front of a bunch of randy cowboys," he said tightly. "A lady doesn't wear pants!"

"Wiggling my . . ." Becca sputtered. "You are despicable, Mr. Ironbow."

"Slade.'"

"Dammit, you're infuriating!"

He lifted one shoulder in a shrug. "A lady doesn't swear, either, so I suppose the pants are, as you say, appropriate. Eat your breakfast." He redirected his attention to his plate.

"Now, you listen to me," Becca said, leaning toward him. "You have no right to make comments about what I wear when I—"

"What happened to the horses your father and Frank were riding when they went down?" he asked, interrupting her.

She blinked. "What?"

"The horses. Where are they?"

Becca sat back in her chair. "My father's horse broke its leg and had to be destroyed. Frank's is in the barn."

Slade nodded and continued to eat.

"Why?" she asked. "Why do you want to know about the horses?"

"I intend to look at Frank's," Slade said. "Eat up or go hungry. I want to get started."

She glared at him and picked up her fork. The remainder of the meal passed in strained silence. Slade cleaned his plate, put on his Stetson, and stood.

"Let's go," he said.

Becca's gaze slid over him as she drained her coffee cup. Damn the man, she thought. There he stood, towering above her, barking orders like he owned the place . . . and looking so ruggedly handsome, that strange heat throbbed deep within her again. Standing so close to her, so tall, strong, dark, he made her remember the shocking, wanton dreams she'd had the night before. Dreams in which he'd embraced her, kissed her, then reached for the buttons of her dress . . .

"I'm ready," she said, jumping to her feet as she felt her cheeks flush. She strode to the back door. "Thank you for breakfast, Maria," she said as she lifted a white Stetson from a peg by the door. Then she left.

"Slade," Maria said.

"Yes?" He turned to look at her.

"Go easy on her."

"She doesn't belong out there."

"She always rode with her pa."

"There's trouble now."

"She's a Colten, and that means she doesn't run from trouble. She's grieving for her pa, but she won't let you see her tears. Becca is strong in some ways, but needs caring for in others. Try to be patient with her, Slade. She needs you here, but she doesn't want to admit how frightened she is of Folger and what he might do. Surely you can understand pride."

Slade looked at Maria for a long moment, then turned and left the house without a further word.

More than thirty men were gathered outside the barn. Slade could see Becca talking to a short, wiry man, who appeared to be in his fifties. As Slade approached a silence fell over the group. All eyes were riveted on him when he stopped in front of them.

He pushed his Stetson back and studied each man's face, one at a time. Tension hung heavily in the air.

Some men met Slade's scrutiny head-on; others couldn't hold his gaze and stared down at the ground.

"You know who I am," he said finally. "I'm not one for speeches, so listen good. I'm in charge. When I give orders I expect them to be followed, no questions asked. Folger will be stopped . . . my way. The Bonnie Blue and Miss Colten will be protected . . . my way "

He looked at Becca. She opened her mouth as though to speak, then snapped it closed.

"If you have a gun and holster," he went on, "wear it. Check your rifle in the boot of your saddle every morning. Pair up. No man rides alone. If a steer gets away, let it go if your partner isn't free to go after it with you. Cover your backs. Stay alert. If you're mending fences, work one on each side. Fire two shots if you see any sign of trouble, anything that doesn't look right to you. When any of us hear those two shots, we'll drop what we're doing and come. If you don't like what I'm saying, pack your gear and clear out now."

He stopped speaking and tugged his Stetson low again, shadowing his eyes. No one spoke. A few men restlessly shifted their feet; someone cleared his throat. Slade waited. The short man Becca had been talking to stepped forward, and all eyes were trained on him.

"Name's Yancey Perkins, Mr. Ironbow," he said, extending his hand. "I'm mighty glad you're here to take over. These here are a good bunch of boys. They'll follow your orders, or I'll pay 'em off and send 'em on their way. What I'm sayin' is, count me in."

Slade shook Yancey's hand. "Slade will do."

Yancey turned to the men. "So? If you're leaving, do it now. Don't stand around on Bonnie Blue land breathing in Bonnie Blue air unless you're willin' to fight to keep it out of Folger's hands."

"Hell, Yancey," someone said, "the Bonnie Blue is home to most of us. We're not goin' nowhere. Pete here will be my partner on the range. I'll stick so close, you'll think I'm in love with him. Mr. Ironbow . . . um, Slade, I'm in."

Slade nodded.

"And you drifters?" Yancey asked. "Some of you ain't been here long. You goin' or stayin'?"

"I'm staying," a young man said. "I came all the way from Pennsylvania to work on this ranch. That polecat Folger isn't driving me off. I've heard of you, Slade. Word is you're about as fast as they come with that gun, and you've never drawn first on a man. Also heard you do some special work for the President when he asks you."

Becca's gaze flew to Slade, but with the hat shading his face, she couldn't read his expression.

"Well, I don't suppose," the young cowboy went on, "you can talk about special and secret doings for the President and all. Anyway, I'm in. You're honest, I hear tell, and that's all adding up to good enough for me."

"I've been told he's a bounty hunter," Becca heard someone say quietly.

"Naw," the man beside him said in a louder voice. "He's hired private by folks wantin' somebody called out for a fair draw."

Her eyes wide, Becca turned as Bob Smith, a cowboy who'd been at the Bonnie Blue for five years, spat tobacco on the ground.

"Well," he said to the three men around him, "he's fast with that gun, and we need help dealing with Folger. I'm countin' myself lucky that Slade showed up here."

Other men added their agreement. No one started toward the bunkhouse to pack his gear.

"Good bunch of boys," Yancey said to Slade, grinning.

"Thank you," Becca said to the men. "Thank you all very much."

"Your pa was a fine man, Miss Colten," Bob Smith said. "We'll settle this with Folger, don't you worry none."

"Damn straight," Bucky said, puffing out his chest.

Someone whopped him on the back, and he nearly toppled over.

"Yancey," Slade asked, "what work was scheduled for today?"

"Half the men mending fences, half moving a bunch of steers from the south end up over to the north ridge to graze."

"Saddle up, then," Slade ordered. "Pair off. If the number is uneven, do three. No one is alone. Miss Colten goes with me."

Talking among themselves, the men ambled into the barn to saddle their horses, some tipping their hats to Becca as they passed her. She watched them go, then walked over to Slade.

"That went very well," she said, smiling up at him. "I'm pleased. My father would be pleased, too, to know they were all loyal to the Bonnie Blue."

Slade looked down at her, and felt his heart instantly beat faster. Lord, she was beautiful. It was the first time he'd seen her smile like that. Her eyes were warm, and those lips . . . Damn, it was sweet torture just to look at Becca's lips. To imagine kissing them . . .

Becca's smile faded, replaced by a frown. She cocked her head to one side as she studied Slade's scowl.

"Why are you so angry?" she asked. "Everything went just fine with the men. They'll follow your orders, I'm sure of that."

"I want to speak with Frank," he said, ignoring her question.

She sighed. "All right. He's in the bunkhouse."

She started toward the low, long building. Slade waited for a moment, then caught up with her. They walked in silence as the men came out of the barn and trotted by on their horses. When the last man had disappeared in a cloud of dust, Slade glanced down at Becca.

"They're loyal to the Colten name," he said, "not just the Bonnie Blue."

She looked up at him in surprise. "What a nice thing to say."

He chuckled. "I'm a nice person once or twice a year."

Heaven help her, Becca thought, nearly forgetting to breathe. Slade's smile softened his stern, rugged features, and even warmed the cold depths of his eyes.

"You have a marvelous smile," she said, hoping her voice was steady. "You should use it more often."

He shrugged. She pulled her gaze from his and reached for the handle to the bunkhouse door. Slade moved at the same moment, and his hand closed over hers.

Heat from his hand seemed to envelop Becca, and she again forgot to breathe. There was such strength in his big hand, she thought, staring at it, and such gentleness, too.

Her hand was so small, Slade thought, seeing it disappear beneath his. And fragile and soft. He'd have to be careful with her, very gentle as he peeled away her clothes—

He jerked his hand away with a smothered curse. "Open the door," he said gruffly.

Becca yanked on it. "You change moods so fast, no one could begin to keep up."

"Don't try."

"I don't intend to." She shot him a cool look, then stalked into the building.

The large bunkhouse was divided into two sections, one for sleeping, one for eating. Wooden tables were lined in rows, and two men were cleaning away the debris from breakfast. Becca smiled at them, then turned to the left and crossed the room.

"Frank?" she called outside a closed door. "It's Becca. May I come in?"

"You bet," a voice answered.

She opened the door and entered the sleeping area,

with Slade right behind her. The room was neat, each bunk made up. Against one wall were round tables for playing cards, and several worn but comfortable chairs sat by a small bookcase containing several much-read books and newspapers. Frank's bed was the nearest to the door. As foreman of the ranch, he had a partition that afforded him some privacy.

"Hello, Frank," Becca said, stopping at the foot of the bed. "How's the leg?"

"Giving me fits." Frank shifted his gaze to Slade. "Howdy, Slade. Damn glad to hear you're taking charge around here."

Slade narrowed his eyes as Becca glanced quickly between the two men.

"You know Slade?" she asked Frank.

"Yep," he said. "I can tell he doesn't remember me, though."

Frank who? Slade wondered, searching his mind. About forty, the foreman was well-built and good-looking, with curly brown hair. Frank. Frankie . . .

"Frankie Tatum," he said, grinning. "Seven, eight years ago, San Antonio."

"You saved my swaggering hide, Slade." He turned to Becca to explain. "I was taking a little side trip after a cattle drive from the Bonnie Blue. I was so drunk I couldn't see, and very convinced that a darlin' saloon gal was in love with me. Never mind that she belonged to Digger McHugh, I was going to have her, by damn."

Slade nodded. "Digger took exception to your choice of women."

"Exception?" Frank said, with a hoot of laughter. Then he groaned and clutched his leg. "Digger was going to shoot me into the next county."

"How lovely," Becca said dryly.

"Slade here stepped in, Miss Colten, even though he didn't know me from Adam. Never saw anyone draw so fast as Slade. He just talked real low, told Digger he was taking me out of there and nobody was going to get hurt. I passed out about then. One of the other men from the Bonnie Blue told me Slade hoisted me over his shoulder while he kept his gun on Digger. He dumped me in a horse trough, I came to, and we rode like blazes out of town. What a night. We made camp and come morning Slade was gone, and I had a headache that I thought would split my head right open. Never did thank you for saving my hide, Slade, so I'm doing it now. Never knew why you bothered, either."

"Digger and I didn't get along very well," Slade said. "I couldn't see letting him kill a man who was too drunk to know his own mind." Slade nodded at Frank's splinted leg. "I see you're still getting into trouble."

"I'm mad as hell about this," Frank said. "Can't figure out why my horse went down. Shouldn't have happened, any more than Jed Colten being thrown. Sorry, Miss Colten, I don't mean to upset you by speaking of your pa."

"That's all right," she said softly. "I'll never believe my father's death was an accident. Your breaking your leg wasn't an accident, either, but there's no proof to the contrary."

"Yet," Slade said.

"Meaning?" Frank asked.

"We'll see. Tell me about Folger."

"He's scum. He was afraid of Jed Colten, but the day of Jed's funeral, Folger got drunk and told anyone who would listen that he was going to make the Bonnie Blue his, that it needed a man to run it. He's thirty-five or six, but soft. Got a drinking belly and doesn't do a lick of work at Four Aces. He hires anyone who's good with a gun. Folger's pa built Four Aces up into a fine spread, but he died of a heart attack two years ago. Henry Folger is letting the ranch slide. He doesn't get a good day's work out of hired guns, but he's hell-bent on having the Bonnie Blue. He's drinking more and more, I hear. He's a dangerous man, Slade, but even drunk he's smart. The sheriff can't pin a thing on him. Folger took care of Jed and me, and there's no telling what he might do next. Damn, I'm mighty glad you're here. Does Folger know?"

"He knows."

"Then watch your back."

"Always do." Slade walked over to a few other bunks and returned with three pillows. Without speaking he carefully lifted Frank's broken leg and positioned the pillows beneath it. "Try that. I'll check in with you later."

"Thanks," Frank said. "Everything is going to be fine, Miss Colten. Slade, if any of the boys give you trouble, send them to me. I'll set them straight about following your orders."

"I don't think there's going to be any problem with the men," Becca said.

Frank looked at Slade for a long moment. "No, I doubt there will be."

"Try to rest, Frank," Becca said, then smiled. "Or is it Frankie?"

"Don't know why I called myself Frankie that night in San Antonio. Fact is, I don't know why I did half of what I did."

"Boys will be boys," Becca said, heading for the door. " 'Bye, Frankie."

"Good day to you, too, Miss Colten," Frank said, smiling.

Slade watched Becca go, then turned back to Frank. "I don't want her out on the range. I've got enough to do without watching over her too."

"She always went out with her pa. Besides, she's better off out there with you than left unprotected in the house. Folger won't bother Maria, I don't figure, but I'd hate to think about Becca being alone with no one but Maria with her."

"You've got a point."

"Folger's a snake in the grass, Slade. Be very careful."

Slade nodded and left the bunkhouse. He found Becca waiting for him outside.

"I want to see Frank's horse," he said.

She nodded. "Small world, isn't it?" she said as they started toward the barn. "You saved Frank's life years ago, and now you meet up with each other again. That was a wonderful thing you did that night in San Antonio."

"I didn't like Digger."

"You saved a man's life. And you're here as a favor to someone else, not because you personally owed my father a debt. You're a very complicated man."

Slade didn't comment.

"Do you really work for the President?"

Slade still didn't comment.

Becca threw up her hands in exasperation. "Is the weather a safe topic? Nice day, isn't it?"

"Yep," he said, a smile tugging at his lips.

She glared at him.

The barn was huge and neat as a pin. There was a place for everything, and everything was obviously in its place. The sweet smell of hay mingled with the aroma of horses, and Slade inhaled the fragrance.

"Frank's horse is in the third stall there," Becca said, pointing

Slade stroked the horse's nose before opening the half-door and entering the stall. He hunkered down, balancing his weight on the balls of his feet, and spoke in a low, steady voice to the animal.

Becca watched the jittery horse calm within moments, and realized that she, too, was nearly mesmerized by the soothing sound of Slade's voice.

Her gaze swept over him, lingering on his strong back, the muscles rippling beneath his shirt as he examined the horse's front legs. Then her gaze lowered to his hard thighs, which his denims molded to perfectly. Heat suffused her, and she quickly looked at his hands instead. He was gently probing the horse's legs. She remembered the feel of his hand closing over hers on the bunkhouse door, remembered its strength, and the heat within her soared.

Slade was magnificent, she thought. In the few hours he'd been at the Bonnie Blue, she felt changed. Her senses had heightened, and everything around her was clearer, sharper, more vivid. Anticipation was building within her, as though Slade was going to reveal some mystery to her. No other man had ever aroused such sensations in her, and she wondered where it would lead . . . with Slade.

"Damn," he said, pushing himself to his feet. His jaw was set in a hard line as he stepped out of the stall and closed the door. "Becca," he asked, stroking the horse's neck, "do you know where Frank went down?"

"Yes."

"Let's saddle up and get out there. I want to have a look around."

She stared at Frank's horse, as though hoping it would tell her what was going on in Slade's mind, then hurried to saddle her own mount.

Six

The morning air was comfortably cool, the sky a brilliant blue. Slade Ironbow riding a horse, Becca decided, was a glorious sight to behold. They moved as one, man and animal, in a graceful flow of beautifully synchronized power.

"Why didn't you name your horse?" she asked after they'd been riding about half an hour. Her own horse was a dappled gray she'd named Misty.

"Why did you name yours?" he countered, glancing at her.

"Well, because . . . she's mine."

"My horse belongs to himself and the wind. He'll stay with me for as long as *he* chooses. Not all Indians believe that, but my father does, and he taught it to me. My mother always named her horses, and my father said that was fine."

"Your mother is a white woman?"

"Was. She died when I was twelve."

"Then you understand the pain of losing a parent, someone you loved dearly."

"Not really," he said dispassionately. "I didn't know my mother very well." He paused. "This is beautiful land on the Bonnie Blue. In fact, it's one of the finest spreads I've seen."

"Thank you," she said absently. Why wouldn't a twelve-year-old boy have known his mother well? she wondered. Where had she been if not with her husband and son? Slade obviously didn't wish to talk about it, and she knew better than to press. All she'd get would be his infuriating silence or one-word answers.

He suddenly reined in his horse, snapping Becca back to attention. She stopped next to him and waited for him to speak.

"Look," he said, gazing off into the distance. "There are miles of wildflowers sweeping up over that rise. I've seen patterned rugs back East, imported from countries like Persia and Turkey, that are symbols of wealth and high social status. But I'd rather have a carpet of wildflowers like that." He took a deep breath. "That's nature's perfume. Nothing is more beautiful."

Becca stared at him intently, a smile slowly curving her lips. Not many men, she mused, shifting her gaze to the rolling fields of vibrant flowers, would stop to look at wildflowers. Slade obviously loved the land and the gifts of nature that came from it. It would take a man such as him to understand her devotion to the Bonnie Blue.

Slade nudged his horse forward, once again pulling Becca from her reverie. A gust of wind swept over them, stirring the dust in its path.

She laughed. "The wind brought a different perfume. The odor of cattle. Personally, I find it heady and rich, but I doubt the people you know in the East would be impressed."

"No, I don't think they would. Becca, did Jed give you a

chance to enjoy the things young girls do, or did he treat you more like a son, bring you out here on the range with him whether you wanted to be here or not?"

"Oh, no, it wasn't like that at all. I pestered him until he gave up and allowed me to ride with him. He insisted I go to school in town and spend time with Maria learning my manners and social graces, but I was always happiest when I was turned loose to ride on the Bonnie Blue.

"I know people are saying I'm destined to be a spinster, especially now that I sent Henry Folger packing. All of my friends are married with a baby or two, but . . ." She shrugged. "I'd like to have a family, but it would be a rare man who would understand and tolerate my love of this land."

Slade nodded. *He* understood. "I move between two worlds: the Indian's and the white man's. I prefer the way of life of my father's people, living off the land. I don't like being in the city for too long at a time. I feel stifled, closed in."

"Yes," Becca said. Slade understood.

They rode in silence for several minutes, the breeze bringing the various scents of flowers and cattle, the musky odor of water holes. Cows bellowed in the distance, adding their voices to the sound of plodding horses' hooves, the buzzing of bees, the occasional shriek of a hawk soaring across the clear blue sky. The sun rose higher in the heavens, adding its warmth to the peaceful scene.

"How did you do with spring calves?" Slade asked, breaking the comfortable silence that had fallen between them.

"Very well. A record number were born, and they're all branded. They'll be ready for the midsummer cattle drive to Houston. My father put his foot down on that, and I was never allowed to go on the cattle drives. Now? We'll see."

"Who handles the paperwork, the records for the ranch?"

She wrinkled her nose. "I do, and it's not my favorite chore, believe me. It keeps me cooped up inside far too long." She paused. "There, up ahead. Frank went down in that wide gap between those two sets of rocks."

When they reached the spot Slade pulled up and swung out of his saddle. He dropped the horse's reins to the ground as Becca tied hers to a mesquite tree.

She looked at his horse. "He won't wander?"

"Not unless he wants to. He's never wanted to."

"One of these days, Mr. Ironbow, you're liable to have a very long walk facing you if that horse has a change of heart."

"Yep." He hunkered down and brushed aside the short, stiff scrub and bunchgrass that grew around the rocks.

"What are you looking for?" she asked.

"What I figure to find."

"In other words, you'll tell me when you're ready to."

"Yep."

Ten minutes passed, then twenty, as Slade went over the area, practically one blade of grass at a time. At last he straightened and climbed the ten-foot rocks on one side of the gap. Again Becca waited, but when he jumped down and climbed the rocks on the other side, she'd had enough and scrambled up after him. He was tracing his fingertip along one rock and nodding. To Becca the rock simply looked like a rock. Then Slade rubbed his finger over a dark splotch staining the gray stone.

"What's that?" she asked.

"Dried blood."

"I guess a small animal was caught here by a larger one."

"No," Slade said, rising.

"No? As in, that's not animal blood? It's human blood?"

He leaned back against the rocks and crossed his arms over his chest. "Frank's horse and, I imagine, your father's went down because of a trip wire."

Her eyes widened. "You're sure?"

"I am about Frank's horse. I'll check the place where your father was killed. The wire was secured on the other set of rocks, and laid on the ground across this gap. A man behind these rocks pulled the wire at just the right moment. In all the confusion no one saw him. No one saw the wire either, because he knew what he was doing. He raised it just enough to do the job. There are thin cuts across the front of Frank's horse's forelegs. They'll heal all right on their own."

Becca's knees weakened. "Dear God," she whispered, "then it's true. My father was murdered, and Frank was intentionally hurt."

"I'll make sure the clues are there concerning your father. Tell me where it happened and I'll come back out on my own. No sense putting yourself through that."

"I want to. I want to see the proof," she said vehemently. "Today. Right now."

"This isn't proof, Becca. It's cause. There's nothing here to link this to Folger."

"Of course it's Folger's work. He hired whoever did this."

"I'm sure he did."

"Well?"

"The man made one mistake. To pull the trip wire, you wrap it around the palm of your hand. A horse hitting that wire carries a lot of weight, and a smart man wears two pairs of heavy work gloves. This blood says that man didn't. Somewhere, there's a man with a deep cut across the palm of his hand."

"It's one of Folger's men, I know it is. Slade, the evidence of the trip wire is proof. It is, don't you see?"

"We can't ride onto Folger's land and demand to examine all of his men's hands."

"There must be *something* we can do."

"Tell our boys to keep their eyes open, whenever they're

in town, for someone with that kind of cut. Don't look so disappointed, Becca. It's a start. We know more than when we woke up this morning. But don't say anything about this to anyone we see today."

"Why not?"

"Because I said so. How far is it to the spot where your father was killed?"

"About a mile north."

"Are you sure you—"

"Yes, Slade, I want to see the proof that my father was murdered. I need to see it, understand?"

"All right. We'll—" His head snapped up, and he stared at a hill in the distance.

Becca looked too. "What is—Oh!"

In a blur of motion, Slade flung himself at her, hurling her to the ground and covering her body with his. Her hat rolled away as a shot rang out, ricocheting off the rocks where Slade had been standing.

"Don't move," he said.

Move? she thought in a rush of panic. She couldn't even breathe. The wind had been knocked out of her, and Slade was lying on top of her. His warm, tightly muscled body was pressed against hers. She could feel his heat, smell the aroma of sweat and leather and the unique scent that was pure male. She was staring at his throat, but then he tipped his head down to look at her, and she was gazing at his lips, so close to hers.

Their eyes met. Becca's heart beat wildly, and she wondered if it was from fear because someone had shot at them, or because she was lying beneath Slade Ironbow. He felt wonderful, heavy and male, rugged and taut . . .

Move, Ironbow! Slade yelled silently at himself. But Becca felt so good. She was shielded by the rocks. There was no excuse for him to keep her pinned to the ground, but she was gazing at him with those big green eyes. . . .

Slade didn't move. Becca didn't move. They continued

to stare at each other. Time lost meaning, and neither could have said if seconds or hours passed. Everything was still, quiet, and Becca was certain Slade would hear the rapid beating of her heart.

Nervously, she slid her tongue along her bottom lip.

Slade groaned, "Damn." Then lowered his head to claim her mouth with his.

Becca's eyes widened in shock, but in the next instant, her lashes drifted down. Her arms encircled Slade's neck, and he deepened the kiss. His tongue parted her lips with gentle insistence and delved into her mouth, and she complied willingly.

Shifting most of his weight to his forearms to keep from crushing her, Slade held her head in his hands. His tongue stroked hers in a rhythmic, seductive duel. The lips that had tortured him were now his. Heat gathered low in his body and his manhood swelled, straining against his pants and pressing into Becca's softness. He ached. He wanted. He burned with a need he'd never known before. All of her passion was desire now, not anger, and it was directed at him. She was responding totally to him in her innocence. Her innocence . . .

Slade fought against the haze of desire clouding his mind. He was losing control, and he never lost control. Not in anger, and sure as hell not in desire. Dammit, what was this woman doing to him!

He tore his mouth from hers, and in one jerky motion rolled off her and away. Drawing his knees up and draping his arms over them, he stared straight ahead, struggling to control his breathing, to control the aching want of his throbbing manhood.

Becca blinked, missing Slade's heat, his weight, the feel of his lips and tongue. Sitting up, she became aware of her trembling limbs, and aware of a curling, pulsing warmth deep within her. She looked at Slade from beneath her lashes. Tension seemed to emanate from him in waves.

"Slade?" she whispered, her voice quivering.

"That shouldn't have happened," he said harshly.

She frowned in confusion. "Why not?"

Slade snapped his head around to look at her. Desire still flushed her cheeks, her lips were swollen, and her eyes were smoky green with passion. His muscles tightened as he forced himself not to move, not to reach for her and claim those lips again. If he touched her now, he wouldn't stop until she was naked beneath him and he was burying his aching manhood deep inside her silken heat.

"Why not?" he repeated, with a sound of disgust. "Do you have any idea how close I came to taking you right here in the dirt?" He paused. "No, you don't know, do you? You're as innocent as a newborn babe. Hell."

"I certainly am not," she said indignantly. Oh, yes, she was, she admitted to herself. She'd been kissed a total of three times before today. Chaste little kisses pressed onto her lips by young men who'd taken her for an outing. Kisses that had left her disappointed. So, she *was* terribly innocent, but Slade Ironbow didn't have to be crude about it. "I'm a twenty-one-year-old woman, Mr. Ironbow," she said stiffly. "One does not live for twenty-one years without a certain amount of . . . experience in these matters."

"Now, is that a fact?" he asked dryly. "Well, good. Take off your clothes."

Her eyes widened. "What?"

He whirled and gripped her shoulders, hauling her up with him. "You felt me, didn't you?" he said, his voice ominously low. "You felt me hard against you, ready to have you. I want you. I ache with wanting you. Are you ready, Becca?" He reached for the top button of her shirt. "I'll do it for you, take off your clothes. Then I'll bury myself deep inside you and make love to you until the sun goes down. That will be fine with you, because you're so experienced in these matters."

"I . . . No, I've never . . . That is, I haven't . . ."

"Dammit," he roared, releasing her. "I know you haven't. I repeat—this should never have happened, and it won't happen again. I'm a man, not a boy. You'd best remember that. Don't kiss men the way you kissed me, Becca Colten, or you're going to get more than you bargained for. Now, stay here while I check for that gunman. In case you've forgotten, someone took a shot at us. Don't move one damn inch."

Becca opened her mouth, but before she could speak, Slade had disappeared around the rocks. She sighed and closed her mouth, realizing she wouldn't have known what to say anyway. She felt like a child, a naive, innocent child. She reached for her hat and plunked it on. Then again, she reasoned, she'd excited and aroused a man like Slade, so she must have kissed him as a woman would have. There was nothing childish about what she'd felt deep inside herself.

She tapped a fingertip against her chin. She should be ashamed of her behavior, she supposed, but she wasn't. Slade was obviously angry as blue blazes at her, but she wasn't angry at herself, nor sorry she'd kissed him. It had felt right, special, and if she could push back time and make the choice, she'd do it all again.

Because it was Slade.

It seemed to Becca that Slade had no sooner left than he returned, startling her out of her reverie.

"You weren't gone long," she said as he hunkered down beside her.

He glared at her. "I'd be breaking my own rules. I can't leave my . . . partner."

"Oh, that's right," she said sweetly. "And I'm your partner. Tsk, tsk, to think that you almost went off and left me all by my lonesome self."

"You're acting strange," he said, peering closely at her.

"Me? Don't be silly. You look like a brewing storm, so I decided someone has to be cheerful in this . . . partnership. Did you see anyone out there?"

"No. I made myself visible to give him another chance to shoot at me, but nothing happened. I figure he's long gone."

"You made yourself visible? So he could shoot at you? That doesn't sound very bright."

"My choices were limited," he said dryly. He pushed himself to his feet and extended his hand to her. "Let's go."

She placed her hand in his and allowed him to pull her to her feet. They were standing toe to toe, and she looked up at him, aware that he still held her hand.

"I'm not sorry, Slade," she said softly, "about what happened. You can holler your head off from here to Sunday, and I still won't be sorry."

He smiled. "I don't holler."

"You certainly do. You growl, too."

His dark eyebrows shot up. "Growl?" he repeated, releasing her hand.

"Yes. Growl."

His smile faded. "Becca, I was more angry at myself than at you. I should never have kissed you, because . . ." He took off his Stetson, raked his hand through his hair, then thrust his hat back on his head. "Let's go."

"Slade, wait." Placing her hand on his arm, she felt him flinch, his muscles tautening beneath her touch. "Can't we talk about this? Why do you feel you shouldn't have kissed me?"

"Dammit, Becca . . ."

"Why?" she asked, tightening her grip.

"I shouldn't have kissed you because I *wanted* to kiss you!" He jerked his arm free and started down the rocks. "Let's go. Now!"

Becca stared up at the sky. "He shouldn't have kissed me, because he *wanted* to kiss me," she repeated under her breath. "Therefore, he's angry because he kissed me. Heavens, what a complicated man."

"Becca!"

"I'm coming," she called, and scrambled down the rocks after Slade.

A short time later, Slade was once more carefully examining the shrub grass between two large sets of rocks. Becca had led him to the area where her father had been killed, and she stood quietly by the horses, watching.

It didn't take him long to find the evidence. He walked back to Becca, unable to keep his gaze from sliding over her, unable to keep from remembering how she had felt beneath him. Unable to forget how much he still wanted her.

"Slade?" she asked as he drew near. "What did you find?"

"Come on," he said gently, "let's get you out of here."

"No, tell me, please."

"It was a trip wire, Becca. Your father . . . was murdered."

She nodded, unable to speak as tears closed her throat. She mounted her horse and fiddled with the reins, not meeting Slade's gaze.

"Are you all right?" he asked quietly.

She nodded again. "Yes. I sensed it. I've never believed it was an accident. There's just something about actually hearing you say the words . . ." She paused to take a breath, then lifted her gaze to his. "I swear to heaven that Folger is going to pay for this. He's going to pay, Slade."

"He will, but you're going to have to be patient." He swung into his saddle. "We'll ride fence for a while now,

see how the men are doing. Remember, don't say anything about us finding out about the trip wires."

"All right."

"Becca."

"Yes?"

"We'll get Folger."

"But what if we can't prove anything? What if—"

"We'll get him," Slade interrupted, a steely edge to his
voice. "You have my word on that." He turned his horse
and started away.

"Thank you, Slade Ironbow," Becca whispered, then
nudged her horse to catch up with him.

Seven

In Dodge City, Kansas, people stood motionless on the wooden sidewalks, watching Doc Willis. He rode straight down the center of the dusty main street in a black buggy with a fancy top edged in fringe, a white horse pulling it.

When he halted in front of the Silver Spur, a collective gasp went up from the women. The men had a variety of reactions. Some nodded in approval, a few smiled enviously, and others shook their heads as they pictured Doc lying dead in the street after Slade Ironbow returned.

Doc jumped down from the buggy, tied the horse's reins to the hitching post, and strode forward to knock at the closed doors of the Spur.

Abe opened one of the doors. "Lord Almighty, you're back."

"I surely am," Doc said, smiling. "I've come calling on Miss Muldoon, Abe. I'd appreciate your letting me in, then informing her that I'm here."

Abe stuck his head out the door and glanced up and down the street. Then he looked at Doc again, grinning.

"I'll inform Miss Muldoon of your arrival, sir," Abe boomed, "and see if she will receive a gentleman this afternoon."

Someone on the street cackled with laughter.

Doc swept off his Stetson and stepped inside. "Gentleman?" he asked Abe.

Abe shrugged as he shut the door. "Lordy, you do have this town in a frenzy. Them chocolates—"

"Doc!"

Doc and Abe looked up to see Mattie hurrying down the stairs. She was wearing a pale green cotton day dress, and tortoiseshell combs held her auburn curls in an attractive, casual tumble on top of her head.

She was absolutely lovely, Doc thought. Whether she was wearing a simple frock or silk and feathers, she was the most beautiful woman in the world.

"Doc . . ." Mattie began, stopping in front of him.

"Jim," he said, smiling warmly at her. "Hello, Mattie. You're looking especially nice today. I've come calling to ask you to go on a picnic lunch with me."

Her eyes widened. "A picnic?"

"Yes, ma'am." He rocked back and forth on the balls of his feet, a very pleased expression on his face. "I have a fine lunch in a wicker basket out in the buggy. I'd be honored if you'd come with me."

"I've never been on a picnic," she said wistfully, then she blinked. "No, I can't. People will talk. They'll—"

"They'll be wishin' *they* was goin' on a picnic," Abe said. "Surely is a fine day for it."

"It is, indeed," Doc said.

"Well, I do need to talk to you . . ." Mattie shook her head. "No, absolutely not. Since you're obviously not using the two cents worth of brains God gave you, Jim Willis, then I'll have to do it for you. You're making the biggest mistake of your life, and I won't be a party to it. I will *not* walk through that door with you, and have the whole town see us leaving together to go on a picnic."

"You're a strong, stubborn woman, Mattie," Doc said. "I know when I'm beat. Abe, if you'll be so kind as to go out to the buggy and get the picnic basket, Mattie and I will have our lunch right here inside the Spur."

"Sure thing," Abe said, starting toward the door.

"No!" Mattie yelled. "Abraham, don't you move another inch." Abe stopped and looked at her, his eyebrows raised questioningly. "Doc . . . Jim, you can't stay in here while the Spur is closed. People will assume that we're . . . I want you to leave right this minute."

"Now, Mattie," Doc said, "as much as I'd like to grant your every wish, it's only fitting that I have a say in our relationship, too. You said you wouldn't go on a picnic with me, so the picnic is coming in here. Seems to me that is a fair give-and-take bargain. It is also my final word on the subject."

"You're crazy," she exclaimed. "You can't stay in here now."

"Then I suggest we proceed with the original plan, and have our picnic outside in the sunshine." He crooked his arm. "Miss Muldoon? Shall we go? We'll talk during lunch. You did say you needed to speak to me, didn't you?" He lifted her hand and placed it on his arm. "Abraham, take charge of the Spur."

"Oh, yes, sir," Abe said, chuckling. "Don't be givin' this place another thought. Enjoy your picnic."

"We certainly will," Doc said.

"But . . ." Mattie began, then shook her head and closed her mouth. Outside, she glanced down the street. "Oh, Jim," she whispered, "everyone is staring. I knew it. I just knew it would be like this."

"Hold your head up high, Mattie Muldoon," he said sternly. "Are you going to let some nosy gossips spoil the first picnic you've ever been on?"

She looked at him for a long moment, then lifted her chin. "No, I'm not." Her eyes sparkled as she saw the buggy and white horse. "Oh, what a fine buggy. I've never ridden in anything so nice-looking."

Doc assisted her onto the seat, then joined her. Once again he rode straight down the middle of the street. Mattie kept her head high, training her eyes on one of the horse's ears. They were at last out of Dodge and away from the buzzing crowd, and she sank back against the seat with a sigh.

"Doc . . . Jim . . . I'm going to say this again. You're making a terrible mistake. I had to speak to you about this. Maybe it's not too late. Maybe. If you stop this foolishness right now, the town folks might forget in time, and your reputation won't be ruined."

Doc turned the horse onto a narrow dirt road and kept going.

"Are you listening to me, Jim?"

"Look at those spring wildflowers," he said. "Fields of them in every color of the rainbow. Now, that is a pretty sight."

"James Willis, you're *not* listening to me!"

"No."

"You sound like Slade," she said, unable to contain a bubble of laughter. " 'Yep' and 'No' are his two favorite words."

"Yep," Doc said, and grinned at her.

Her smile faded, and she sighed. "Oh, Jim, how can I make you understand that this is wrong, and hopeless?"

"You can't. I love you, Mattie."

He reined in the horse beneath a large tree and jumped down from the seat. After securing the reins to a branch, he came around to her side and extended his arms to her.

She placed her hands on his shoulders as he gripped her waist and lifted her off the seat to the ground. He didn't release her, nor did Mattie drop her hands from his shoulders.

They stood there in the shade of the tree, surrounded by wildflowers that filled the air with a delicate fragrance. Bees hummed, birds chirped and sang, a sassy squirrel chattered.

Jim dipped his head and covered Mattie's lips with his.

All thoughts and fears fled Mattie's mind as her lashes drifted down. She was instantly swept away to the rosy place that only Jim could take her to. She returned his kiss with all of her love, feeling safe and protected in the circle of his arms.

He slowly lifted his head. "Let's . . ." He cleared his throat. "Let's get our picnic lunch." He drew his thumb lightly over her lips before reaching for a blanket and the wicker basket that were tucked behind the seat. "There's a nice group of trees over there."

Mattie nodded, unable to speak. Her knees were trembling from the passionate kiss, her heart was racing. She walked through the flowers at Jim's side in silence.

They ate in silence, too, their picnic of fried chicken, biscuits, and fresh fruit. At last Doc pushed his food away and took Mattie's hand.

"Do you believe that I love you?" he asked.

"Yes," she said softly.

"Do you . . . care for me at all? I mean, do you feel *something* for me? Please, tell me the truth. You kiss me as though you do, but I need to hear the words."

She looked away, her eyes misting with tears.

"Mattie?"

"Whatever I may or may not feel for you isn't important."

"Yes, it is! If you love me, then together we can do anything. Nothing can stop us from finding our happiness. Oh, Mattie, please, say the words, tell me that what I see in your eyes, feel in your kiss is true."

"No," she said, shaking her head. "No, I . . . don't . . ." The tears spilled onto her cheeks. ". . . don't love you, Jim."

He gently cradled her face in his hands, stroking away her tears with his thumbs. "Is that a fact? Then why the tears, my Mattie? Why the sadness I see in your beautiful green eyes? You say that you don't love me? Well, Mattie Muldoon, I say that you do."

"No!"

"Oh, yes, and your love is very precious to me. I won't let you go, Mattie. I've waited a lifetime for you, and I have no intention of losing you now."

"Why won't you listen to me?" she cried, pulling his hands from her face. *"I don't love you."*

"Have another piece of chicken. It really is delicious."

"You are the most maddening man on the face of this earth, Dr. Willis." She crossed her arms over her breasts. "Even if I loved you, it wouldn't change anything. We're from different worlds, Jim, don't you see that? People just wouldn't allow us to live in peace. You can tell me that you don't care what they say, and maybe you wouldn't . . . at first. But in time, when folks no longer treated you with the respect they once did, you'd come to regret marrying me. The people in Dodge are narrow-minded. They'll refuse to come to you; they'll go to your assistant instead. You'll be shunned, lose the practice you've worked so hard and long for. You know what I'm saying is true, but you just don't want to face it. It might not be too late, if you stop seeing me. Oh, Jim, people are . . . are . . . well, the way they are."

He smiled at her. "I know that. Old Mrs. Kennedy was in my office this morning for her cough syrup and pretended I was invisible. She spoke to my assistant as though I wasn't in the room, then flounced out the door with her nose in the air. It was quite a performance." He chuckled softly.

Mattie's eyes widened. "And you think it's funny? How much more proof do you need to be convinced that you're making a terrible mistake? Mrs. Kennedy is only the beginning of the trouble you're bringing on yourself."

"I'm very aware of that," he said, his smile gone. "It would be nice to think that people will come around in time, but they won't. As you said, people are the way they are. I'm courting you in the open, making my intentions clear to prove to *you* how much I love you. And I do love you, and I truly believe that you love me, no matter what you say. That means we'll stand together in whatever we decide to do. We can stay in Dodge and ignore the people who snub us. Or . . ."

"Or?"

"We can leave, start fresh someplace else. We could go to California. There are new towns springing up all over the place out there. But I would never ask you to give up the Silver Spur if you didn't want to leave it. If my medical practice dies in Dodge, I'll work at the Spur. See, Mattie? Choices. Together, we can do whatever we please."

"And if we moved to California?" she asked. "What would I do? Open another house of pleasure?"

"You would do whatever made you happy."

"It would be the same as Dodge. The doctor and the saloon girl. Our reputations would catch up, if they didn't beat us to California. People won't accept me."

"I think they would if that was our choice. Back when Dodge was new, people were much more tolerant of each other, because they shared a common bond of struggling to make a start in a rough, new country. Mattie, don't dwell on these choices anymore today. It's a lot to digest all at once. We'll sort them through, decide what is best later."

She looked at him for a long moment, then began to pack the food back into the basket. "Perhaps it's time you heard something that will convince you you've chosen poorly in loving me. Something that will cause your love to die."

"Nothing could cause that to happen, Mattie."

"Slade's in Texas," she said, not looking at him.

"Oh? I didn't think he ever told you where he was going when he left."

"I asked him to go there." She closed the lid of the basket and ran her finger over the woven wicker, then slowly lifted her eyes to meet Doc's. "I needed his help because my—my daughter is in trouble."

"Your daughter?" he echoed, obviously surprised.

"Yes, my daughter. You were in Dodge when Becca was born. You were working with that old doctor, and I can remember seeing you around town. I didn't have the money to send for the doctor when my time came and . . ." She drew a shaking breath. "I guess I should start at the beginning."

He set the basket off the blanket and moved closer to her, taking one of her hands in his.

"I'm from Ohio," she began. "My father . . ."

Mattie continued to speak in a low voice, staring off into the distance. Doc's gaze was riveted on her face as he listened to her story.

"And so," she finished, her voice choked, "Slade has gone to the Bonnie Blue. I don't know how great the danger is there, or what's happening to them. I . . ." She met Jim's gaze. "I gave my baby to Jed Colten. I gave her away."

"You loved her," he said gently. "You did the best thing for her. Oh, God, Mattie, I'm so sorry you suffered such pain. To think I was in Dodge then and never even knew you. I didn't go to the Spur much, didn't pay any attention until it was suddenly turned into the fanciest place in town, and you were the owner."

"And Slade's woman."

"I believed that." He smiled. "Everyone still does. Very clever, Miss Muldoon."

"Jim, I had a child. You spoke of wanting a baby. What can you think of a woman who gave hers away?"

"You were hardly more than a child yourself. I think

you have a heart overflowing with love. Slade saw that in you. And what you've just told me convinces me that I've chosen well. You're a strong, loving, wonderful woman. Oh, Mattie, I really love you."

He kissed her, and Mattie swallowed a sob as she wrapped her arms around his neck and clung to him. She pulled him closer, needing his warmth and strength to quiet the voices of the past and bring her back to the present.

Doc gently lowered her to the blanket, his mouth never leaving hers. The kiss deepened with his desire to banish her ghosts, to take her from the pain of her past and into a future of happiness with him. As he felt her tension ebb and her passion rise, he gentled the kiss to a sensual embrace.

At last he lifted his head. "You're mine now," he said, his breathing rough. "I can't change the past, but I can have a voice in the future. We'll be together, Mattie. Nothing will ever hurt you again. I love you."

She stared at him for a long moment, then abruptly shoved him away, struggling to sit up. "Please take me back into town, Jim. There's nothing more to be said between us, because you refuse to listen to me. I pray that you'll come to your senses before your reputation is totally ruined. I do *not* love you, James Willis."

A slow smile crept onto Doc's face, then widened into a grin. "You're the most beautiful liar I've ever seen." He got to his feet and extended his hand to her. "Miss Muldoon, I shall escort you home."

Mattie sighed with frustration, then placed her hand in his.

Eight

Slade stepped out of the stall and closed the half-door. Becca was tending to her horse, and he saw her smile at the men who were entering the barn. She laughed as two complained about it being their turn to muck out the stalls, and his body tightened at the sound of the rich, throaty resonance dancing through the air.

Memories of kissing her flitted through his mind. Her body had been so soft beneath his . . . He pushed the vivid pictures away, and roughly tugged his Stetson down on his forehead.

"I want to see everyone outside when you've tended to your horses," he said gruffly, then strode from the barn and away from Becca Colten.

Outside, Slade glanced at the sky. The first streaks of the sunset tinted its blue with purple, orange, and yellow. He filled his lungs with the cool air, then leaned against the barn, crossing his arms over his chest.

He had to admit Becca had done well that day. They'd

covered a lot of ground checking on the men, but she'd never complained about the pace he set.

He'd spoken to her only occasionally, and she'd answered his questions with obvious knowledge of the workings of the Bonnie Blue. She hadn't pressed him to talk to her, nor had she blathered on about nonsensical things the way so many women he knew did. Her love of the land was apparent, and he respected that.

He had felt a sense of pride himself as they'd ridden over the Bonnie Blue. Pride that wasn't his to possess. The emotion had startled him, for the Bonnie Blue wasn't his. It was Becca's.

As the men gathered, talking among themselves, smoking, laughing, Becca walked over to Slade.

"Everyone is here," she said.

"Yancey," Slade said, "call the cooks out here."

"Sure thing, Slade."

When the cooks appeared, everyone looked at Slade. He stayed where he was, appearing completely relaxed.

"Those of you I saw today," he said, "know that someone took a shot at me and Miss Colten. Folger is not happy, it would seem, that I'm here. That's fine. We're shifting the deck, creating nervousness at Four Aces instead of here."

The men nodded.

"I found evidence today," Slade went on, "that Jed Colten's horse, and Frank's, went down because of trip wires."

"Damn that Folger," someone yelled over the mutterings of the men. "Damn his murdering hide."

Slade glanced at Becca. She was standing a few feet away from him, her hands clutched tightly together. He raised a hand for silence and pushed himself away from the barn.

When the men quieted, Slade explained about the dried blood he'd found, and the need for the men to watch for someone with a deep cut on the palm of his hand. The injury wasn't going to be that easy to spot, he added, as cowboys from habit often wore their gloves beyond working hours. More than half of the men of the Bonnie Blue still had their gloves on.

"We know," he said, "that Folger is clever, despite the fact that he drinks heavily, but the odds are that he'll make a mistake. Continue riding in pairs, and remember to check your guns every morning. We have to be patient and stay alert. That's all I have to say for now."

The men broke up into groups, talking among themselves as they waited for the clang of the supper bell.

Becca turned toward the house, then glanced back at Slade. He was once more leaning against the barn, seeming to be relaxing after a long, tedious day in the saddle. Though he appeared to be half-asleep, she sensed the coiled readiness in his taut, muscled body.

Unnerved that she could so easily read his moods, she strode on to the house.

In her room she shut the door and leaned against it, closing her eyes. The events of the day came rushing back, tumbling together in her mind. She pressed her fingertips to her aching temples in an attempt to still the vivid scenes.

At last she drew a deep, calming breath, opened her eyes, and slowly removed her clothes. With sheer force of will, she blanked her mind and washed in the china bowl before putting on a clean chemise, then brushing her hair. As she reached for her mourning dress, she hesitated, then turned, gave a weary sigh, and stretched out on the bed.

"Oh, Pa," she whispered, tears filling her eyes. "Folger took you from me, and he's got to pay. I can't bring you back, but Folger isn't going to get away with this. Slade will see to it . . ."

She stopped speaking and dashed away the tears that

had fallen onto her cheeks. Speaking Slade's name brought back the memory of the taste and feel of his mouth on hers. Heat fluttered deep within her. This was the desire of a woman, she thought, brought to life by Slade's touch. Of that she was certain.

But what she didn't know was if she was falling in love with Slade Ironbow.

Sighing again, she slid off the bed. After dressing and tying her hair back with a black ribbon, she left the bedroom. At the bottom of the stairs she turned left, then faltered when she saw Slade leaning nonchalantly in the doorway leading to the dining room. He was watching her approach, and the heat of his gaze seemed to sear the fabric of her dress. She moved forward slowly, her gaze skimming his tall, rugged body, then boldly meeting his eyes.

Memories of the kiss shared at the rocks rushed over her once again, and her knees began to tremble. She had a sudden and rather frightening urge to run to Slade, to fling herself into his arms and press her lips and body to his. She forced herself to walk sedately, her chin held high, her eyes meeting his unflinchingly.

Slade hoped that he appeared relaxed. If the truth be known, every muscle in his body was tensed as he held himself in check. The urge to haul her into his arms and smother her mouth with his was gnawing at his gut. Never had he wanted a woman as he did Becca Colten.

Becca stopped in front of him. His face was expressionless, and she adopted what she hoped was a bland expression of her own.

"Shall we have supper?" she asked, damning the thread of breathlessness in her voice.

He inclined his head and swept one arm in the direction of the dining room. "After you, ma'am."

"Thank you." She swooshed into the room with a dramatic flair that she knew wasn't necessary, but it was better than leaping into the man's arms and making a complete fool of herself.

Slade pulled out her chair at the head of the table. "Ma'am?" he said, bowing.

"You're most kind." She sank gratefully onto the seat as the quivering in her knees increased.

Slade tightened his hold on the back of the chair, unable to tear his gaze away from her straight back, the tiny waist, her gently curved hips and bottom, that had been so enticingly outlined by the pants she'd worn. Resisting the urge to touch her, he dropped his hands from the chair and took his place next to her.

Steaming platters of food were already on the table, and Slade reached for the potatoes, not speaking as he ladled a hefty serving onto his plate. Becca began to fill her own plate.

The silence in the room was deafening, broken only by the clink of spoons and forks against china dishes. There was a nearly tangible entity in the room with them, a crackling tension, a sexual awareness. They ate without speaking, neither tasting, nor even wanting, the food.

At last Slade shoved his empty plate away and got to his feet. "I have things to do," he said gruffly, and strode from the room with long, heavy strides.

"Well!" Becca said indignantly. She plunked one elbow on the table and rested her chin in her hand. "Well," she repeated.

She sat staring at the doorway until Maria startled her by coming into the dining room to clear away the dishes.

Slade left the house to find that dusk had turned to night. He took a thin cigar from the pocket of his shirt and lit it with a wooden match. Inhaling deeply, he wandered over to a corral where a stallion was grazing.

Fine animal, he mused as he rested his arms on the top

slat of the enclosure. There was some good breeding stock on the Bonnie Blue. He puffed on the cigar. Becca would give a man a fine son. Slade chuckled softly. Oh, Becca would spit fire if she knew he was standing there comparing her to good breeding stock!

Slade looked at the glowing end of the cigar. He really didn't want it, he decided, and ground it out in the dirt with the heel of his boot.

What would it be like to have a son, he wondered. A child created by him and a special woman. He'd saddened his father when he hadn't taken a wife years before and produced an heir to carry on the name of Ironbow. But loving a woman, Slade had determined long ago, would mean having to choose between his two worlds, and he wasn't prepared to do that.

He scanned the horizon, illuminated in the moon-bright night. Becca loved the Bonnie Blue, but she couldn't run it alone, not even with the loyal men working there. The ranch needed a strong man, a man who loved the land, respected it, gave to it as much as he took.

Slade stiffened and shook his head as if to clear it. He wasn't making sense again, dammit. He'd been picturing himself running the Bonnie Blue with Becca; had seen himself making love to her, watching her grow big with his child. He could even see her in his father's camp, laughing, talking, enjoying the chance to learn of a different culture.

No! he thought fiercely. He was as free as the wind.

And no one captured the wind.

He was alone.

Slade rubbed a hand across his face. Alone. Why did that sound so empty?

"Hey, Slade," a man called.

Startled, Slade whirled to see Pete walking toward him. He'd been so wrapped up in his thoughts, he hadn't heard the man approach. A great protector he made, he thought wryly.

"We're going to play a little poker," Pete said, stopping beside Slade. "Want in?"

"No, I . . ." I what? Slade asked himself. Would rather be alone? "Yeah, Pete, I'm in." Maybe he'd get a short reprieve from the tormenting images of Becca Colten.

Weather in the Texas Panhandle was extremely unpredictable. By dawn the next day the sky was heavy with dark rain clouds, and a chill wind forced everyone to don jackets or ponchos.

Becca wore a bright blue wool poncho that Maria had made for her on the treadle-operated sewing machine Jed had purchased the year before. Slade shrugged into a jacket of soft deerskin lined with lamb's wool.

"That's a beautiful jacket," Becca said, as they led their horses from the barn.

"Thank you," Slade said. "It was made for me by a woman named Morning Mist in my father's camp."

"Oh." What else had the woman with the beautiful name done for him, she wondered. Then, angry at herself for even thinking about it, she quickened her pace, striding out of the barn ahead of him. His low chuckle followed her.

Nearly all day the rumble of thunder had the cattle bellowing and moaning, as if in reply. The animals were restless, the calves staying close to their mothers. If the clouds would relinquish their gift of rainwater, the cattle would calm and enjoy the downpour. But as the air pressure built, the animals' edginess grew.

The never-ending job of riding fence to look for broken wire was assigned to half the men. The remaining cowboys were to round up a hundred head of cattle and transfer them to a stretch of grazing land several miles away, on the other side of a rise. Slade and Becca were to begin checking both the natural and man-made water holes.

"Slade," Becca said after she and Slade had ridden in silence for almost half an hour, "you've had a look at Satan, the stallion in the corral. I'm breeding him this spring. What's your opinion of him?"

"He's a fine animal. One of the best stallions I've seen."

"My father bought him about six months ago with the idea of increasing our stock of horses, with Satan as the sire."

"It would be a good line with the right mares."

"That's what I think. There aren't enough mares in this area of any worth that the ranchers are willing to sell. I was thinking about buying them in Houston after the cattle drive, then paying some of the boys extra to bring them back here. I'd like to see the Bonnie Blue gain a reputation for having excellent horses to sell, as well as cattle."

Slade smiled at her. "Then do it. Once this trouble with Folger is finished there won't be any reason not to." Becca Colten surely did know about ranching, he thought, and the glow in her eyes reflected her love for the land. She was quite a woman. "There's a water hole coming up. I can smell it," he said.

"I can't. I happen to know there's a water hole over that next hill, but I certainly can't smell it."

"That's because you don't have a part-Indian nose."

"Oh, I see." She laughed. "You're a handy fella to have around. Maybe I'll keep you."

She glanced quickly at Slade, hoping what she had said had passed by him unnoticed. But he was looking directly at her, all traces of his smile gone.

The horses plodded on, oblivious to the sensual tension weaving between Becca and Slade. She was first to break the visual contact, snapping her head back around, and nudging her horse to a canter up the hill. Slade willed his heated body once more under his control, then followed her, his jaw set in a hard line.

"Slade!" she called from the top of the hill. "There's a calf stuck in the mud in the water hole!" She disappeared over the other side.

"Wait until I—Dammit."

Slade arrived to find Becca wading into the murky water. Her horse stood on the edge of the hole, next to the lowing mother of the calf. Becca had draped her poncho over her saddle, and was already waist-deep in water as she spoke in a quiet, soothing voice to the frightened baby. She carried a rope in her hands.

"Toss me the end," Slade said, swinging out of his saddle. "My horse can pull him out."

She slid the rope over the calf's head, then threw the end to Slade. He wrapped it around his saddle horn, and while Becca pushed on the rear end of the calf, he instructed his horse to inch backward. Slowly, the calf worked his way free.

"Oh, hurry up," Becca said, with a moan. "I'm freezing to death in here. Move, little guy."

At last the calf was free and was greeted by its noisy mother. Becca trudged out of the water, wet to her neck and shivering.

Oh, God, Slade thought, his gaze skimming over her. Her shirt was plastered to her, outlining her soft breasts to perfection, revealing nipples taut from the cold. Blood pounded through him as he stared at her. She was wet and muddy, water dripping off her. And she was the most beautiful woman he'd ever seen.

"We'd better get you back to the ranch," he said, his voice unexpectedly rough, "before you catch a chill."

"No. That would leave you out here without a partner."

"Becca, you're going back to the ranch."

She started to retort, then smiled. "All right, Slade. I

have some paperwork to get caught up on. Maria and I will have a lovely day together, just the two of us . . . alone. I certainly hope that Henry Folger doesn't decide to come calling."

Her eyes widened at the expletive Slade muttered, then she resumed her pleasant expression.

"You win," he said gruffly, then spun on his heel and started away. "I'll gather some kindling and get a fire going. We'll stay right here until you dry out and warm up. Don't put your poncho on now. Wait until later."

"Yes, sir," she said sweetly.

He shot her a dark glare over his shoulder, then proceeded to collect kindling. A short time later a small but warming fire was crackling, and the pair sat close to it, their backs against a log Slade had rolled into place. The sky was even darker than before and the wind was biting cold. The fire felt heavenly, Becca thought.

It was as though she and Slade were the only two people on the face of the earth, and there was no world beyond the fire's circle of warmth, scented with the fragrant aroma of mesquite. She was in a safe cocoon with Slade, and there was no place else she wished to be.

There were, however, she mused, a few things she'd like to know about this man she was so drawn to.

"Apparently," she said, adding her voice to the sound of the snapping fire, "there are a lot of rumors circulating about you, about what you actually do and who you do it for."

"Yep."

"Doesn't that disturb you? The fact that people talk about you, and not everything they say can possibly be true?"

"No." He rolled a blade of scrub grass between two fingers. "I know who I am, Becca, and that's what's important. I belong to two worlds, the Indian's and the white man's, and I won't choose one over the other. Who

I am as a man is my business. What people say is of no concern to me."

"Don't you get lonely?"

"Don't you? Most women your age are surrounded by friends, and they don't spend much time out on the range."

"It's where I want to be," she said. "Even if I marry, I won't give up all my hours spent out here. It's where I belong."

"Just as I belong to both of my worlds."

She nodded, and then they fell silent again, lost in their own thoughts.

The next several days were uneventful, with no hint of trouble from Folger. Nor were any of the Four Aces men seen in town. It was quiet, too quiet, as everyone waited, knowing the peace was temporary, but not knowing where, when, or how it would end. And with the waiting, anxiety rose.

Tempers were quick to flare, but apologies came just as fast, as the Bonnie Blue cowboys stood firm in their resolve to beat Folger. They would stick together, like a large family, and win. If only, they muttered among themselves, they had some idea what Folger was up to.

In addition to the tension the clever Henry Folger had created by his silence and inactivity, there was another tension building. It was centered on just two people. Becca and Slade.

They rode side by side during the long hours from dawn to dusk. To the Bonnie Blue men, they gave all appearances of getting on well together. Becca had a smile and cheerful greeting for everyone as she and Slade checked on the men during the day. Slade was his usual quiet, but confidence-building, self.

But Becca was ready to scream in pure frustration.

Slade would have gladly put his fist through any available wall.

While Slade's respect for Becca grew, so did his awareness of her as a woman. The sound of her voice, her laughter, every graceful move she made, tightened the knot of hot desire within him. Every night dreams of Becca plagued his sleep. His mind and body became his enemy during the day as he spent hours by her side.

He would not, he vowed to himself over and over, touch Becca Colten again. She was a spell-weaver, taking hold of thoughts that he once had total control over. He would not succumb to her magic.

But, God, how he wanted her.

Becca yearned for the dawn of each new day so she could escape the prison of her bed, and the nightly dreams of Slade. But with the sunrise came the man himself, and the quickening of her heart at the mere sight of him.

The memories of his kiss, the feel and taste of his lips on hers, refused to dim. Heat would pour through her at the remembrance of his body on hers when he'd flung her to the ground by the rocks.

Throughout the long hours in the saddle she was aware of every inch of his muscled body. They spoke little to each other, but the sound of Slade's rich, deep voice sent shivers coursing through her.

And always there were the taunting questions. Was she falling in love with Slade Ironbow? What were his feelings for her? Was she really hearing a ring of pride in his voice when he spoke of the Bonnie Blue? Was it possible that he might come to love her, and stay there with her for all time?

The hours ticked slowly by.

At the end of the fifth day, Slade made his usual announcement in the barn that he would speak to everyone outside once they'd tended to their horses. He strode away, not looking at Becca. She watched him go before turning to unsaddle her horse.

Outside, a gorgeous sunset streaked across the heavens. Slade didn't notice. He paced restlessly, waiting for the men to gather. Then he groaned as he realized he still had supper to suffer through, sitting across the table from Becca.

The men filed out of the barn. When they were all there, Slade couldn't stop himself from looking for Becca. She stood near him, between Yancey and Bucky.

He pushed his Stetson to the back of his head. "You all know it was another quiet day. Folger is playing this like a poker hand, showing nothing, hoping to rattle us enough to catch us off guard."

"How long you figure he'll do this, Slade?" one man asked. "We're holding up, but it sure does get on a man's nerves."

"That's a fact," another man said. "Every day out on that range seems like a week. I'm waitin', watchin' . . . It's just so damn quiet."

"Slade," Pete asked, "how can Folger know what's going on over here? I guess he wants us jumping at each other, trouble brewing among ourselves, but how's he to know if his plan is doin' the job?"

Slade nodded. "Good question, and I've been giving that a lot of thought." His dark gaze flickered over the men. "It seems to me that there's only one way Folger can keep informed on the doings at the Bonnie Blue. He's getting firsthand reports from someone . . ." He paused, and when he spoke again his voice was ominously low and cold. "You take one more step, cowboy, and it will be your last."

He walked slowly through the group as the men stepped out of his way. He didn't hurry, his gaze riveted on one man who was backing up as Slade advanced.

"What in the hell is he doing?" someone muttered.

"Shut up," the man beside him whispered. "Lord, he's like a cougar stalking his prey. He's after Gil."

"You stay away from me, Indian," Gil said, still retreating. A wild, panicked look swept across his face. "You got no say over me, half-breed."

"Don't think he oughta have said that," Yancey murmured to Becca.

Slade kept on walking in smooth, even strides. "Gil, is it?" he said. "How long you been on the Bonnie Blue, Gil?"

"That's none of your damn business," Gil yelled. "Get away from me."

"Been here 'bout six weeks," Yancey said calmly.

"I'm not following you into the next county, Gil," Slade said. "I think you'd best stop right there."

Gil stopped, looking anxiously at the other men. "Help me. This Indian is crazy. I didn't do nothin'. He's singled me out for no reason. Dammit, get him away from me."

No one moved.

Becca chewed nervously on the inside of her cheek.

Bucky clutched his stomach with both hands.

Yancey smiled.

"I've noticed," Slade said, still advancing, "that you wear your gloves an awful lot, Gil. I even saw you eating supper with them on one night. This is the first time I've seen your hands since I told everyone about the trip wires."

Slade closed the remaining distance between himself and Gil, and his hand snapped out to grab the cowboy's right wrist. Gil's hand was wrapped in a dirty bandage. Slade unwound the cloth, ignoring Gil's yelp of pain and his loud curses.

"Nasty cut," Slade said quietly. "How'd that happen, Gil?"

"Mending fences." He attempted to pull his wrist free,

but Slade tightened his hold. "Everybody gets sliced up by barbed wire."

"That's not a barbed-wire cut. That's from the trip wire. You made a mistake. You should always wear two pair of heavy gloves when you're working a trip wire."

The men surged forward.

"You murdering bastard!" one shouted. "You killed Jed Colten. Let us have him, Slade. We'll settle this."

"No!" Gil yelled. "Ironbow, please, don't turn me over to them."

Slade dropped Gil's wrist. "You said I should get away from you. I think this is as good a time as any to do just that."

"No! They'll kill me, damn you. I was just doing my job, what I'd been paid for."

"Who paid you?" Slade asked.

"Folger!"

"Oh, dear God," Becca whispered, the color draining from her face.

"When are you supposed to report to Folger next?" Slade asked.

"Tonight. I'm expected over there at ten tonight. I just sneak out when everyone is asleep and . . . Don't give me to these men, Slade. Please."

"Let us have him," Pete said. "We got a score to even here."

"No," Becca said. Everyone turned to look at her. "My father wouldn't want it done that way, Pete. We'll bring in the sheriff and do this right. Folger is guilty, but we're not going to stoop to his level. We owe it to my father and to Frank to stay within the law. We owe it to the reputation of the Bonnie Blue."

She was magnificent, Slade thought, staring at her.

"Yeah, yeah," Gil said, nodding frantically. "Turn me over to the sheriff; put me in jail where no one can get to me. I was doing a job, following orders. They can't hang me for that. Folger planned it all. He's the one you want."

Slade frowned. "Folger's word against a drifter's." He shook his head. "Damn."

"I'll tell the sheriff everything," Gil said, a whining tone entering his voice. "I'll swear that Folger hired me to set those trip wires."

"And Folger will deny it," Yancey said. "Brady Webster will be caught in the middle with no proof against Folger. This lowlife will hang, and Folger will be free as a bird."

"Yep," Slade said.

"Are you saying that Folger is going to get away with this?" Becca asked. "With killing my father? Hurting Frank?"

"No," Slade said. "Pete, you and Cody tie Gil up. Tex, set it up for everyone to take turns standing guard over him."

"Consider it done," Pete said.

"What about Brady?" Tex asked. "You bringing him into this? He's an honest sheriff, Slade."

"I'm counting on that. We'll bring him in when we're ready. In the meantime, the fact that we have Gil under wraps doesn't leave this ranch. No one is to know."

"But, Slade," Yancey said, "Folger's expecting Gil over at Four Aces at ten tonight."

"Time for supper," Slade said. "You men take care of Gil, then eat. Miss Colten, it's been a long day. I'm sure Maria has your supper ready. Go on to the house. I'll be along in a bit."

"Oh, no, you don't," Becca said, marching forward. The men jumped out of her way, and she walked right up to Slade, planted her hands on her hips, and glared at him. "You're going to Four Aces at ten o'clock, aren't you? You're going alone to surprise Folger by showing up instead of Gil."

Slade smiled. "I never said that."

"Don't flash that knock-'em-dead smile at me, Slade Ironbow. I'm not some simpering female you can charm your way around. I want a straight answer."

"I wouldn't talk to him like that," Cody said to Yancey, "if you paid me one hundred in gold." Yancey chuckled.

"Well?" Becca said.

"You're a nosy woman, Becca Colten," Slade said, his voice rising.

"And you're an idiot if you go to Four Aces alone, Slade Ironbow," she yelled.

Slade took a deep breath, let it out slowly, and reined in his temper. "I will do this my way," he said through clenched teeth. "Go to the house. Now."

"Fine," she said sweetly. "We'll finish this discussion there." She turned and stomped away.

"This discussion is over," Slade called after her.

"The hell it is, mister," she shot back, continuing on to the house.

Yancey hooted with laughter. Slade shot him a dark look, but Yancey laughed on, thoroughly enjoying himself.

"Hell," Slade muttered. "What's next? Get Gil taken care of, set up the guard schedule, eat your supper."

As the men moved to follow their orders, Yancey strolled up to Slade.

"You really going to Folger's alone tonight?" he asked.

"Yep."

"We'd back you up, Slade, you know that. Every man here would be willing to go with you."

"I know, and so does Folger. He won't believe I came alone. He'll figure you're all out there watching. Doing it my way gets the job done with no risk of anyone getting hurt."

Yancey nodded, approval evident in his expression. "Risky, but makes sense, I guess."

"I just want Folger to know we're one step ahead of him

now," Slade said. "Fill Frank in on what's going on. I suppose I'd better get up to the house."

Yancey cackled. "Becca's got a temper on her, don't she? Always did, even when she was a tiny thing no taller than Jed's knee. They were good together, Becca and Jed."

"What was Mrs. Colten like?"

"Bonnie? Frail, real sickly. Nearly broke Jed's heart when she died, but he pulled himself together for Becca's sake. This has been real rough on Becca, Slade. She surely did love her pa. Becca doesn't look like either Jed or Bonnie, but she's a Colten. Stubborn, temper ready to flare, pride with no end, works hard. She's a fine little gal, that Becca. Jed was mighty proud of her."

"Her mother would be, too," Slade said. Yes, Mattie would be proud.

"Sure thing. You go easy over there at Four Aces tonight, Slade. Let me know when you get back safe."

"Yep."

"Providing, of course, that Miss Becca don't shoot you right now when you walk in the kitchen door."

Slade glared at him and stalked toward the house, Yancey's laughter drifting after him in the gathering dusk.

Nine

Still fuming, Becca strode into her room, splashed water over herself, and hauled on her mourning dress. She tugged her brush through her heavy hair, ignoring the painful prickles from her rough treatment.

"Damn that Slade Ironbow," she muttered, yanking on the brush again. "Ow!"

When she'd realized that Slade was planning on going to Four Aces alone in Gil's place, she had been filled with a chilling fear. As much as she wanted Folger to pay for her father's death, and the Bonnie Blue freed of threat, she couldn't bear the thought of anything happening to Slade. There were over thirty men on the Bonnie Blue who'd be more than willing to go with him and—

And what? she asked herself. Go galloping in to challenge the fast guns Folger had hired? What purpose would that serve other than to have men lose their lives while Folger sat fat and protected in his fancy house?

No, Becca decided, it wouldn't be wise to storm the gates of Four Aces. But it certainly didn't seem overly intelligent for Slade to go alone, either. What was the man using for brains?

"Well," she said, flinging open the bedroom door, "he can just explain to me why he's doing this. This is my ranch, and I deserve to know."

As she marched down the hall, her anger cooled and her steps slowed. Yelling at Slade, she realized, would get her nowhere. He'd just close his mouth, set his jaw, and stare at her with those coal-black eyes of his. She had to keep her temper in check and calmly, quietly ask Slade to explain his reasoning.

In the dining room, she nodded politely to Slade, then they took their places at the table. Maria had made a stew, and they ladled it into their bowls. They ate in silence for several minutes, until Becca could stand no more.

"Slade," she asked, shifting her gaze to him, "why do you want to go to Folger's alone?"

He took another spoonful of stew and swallowed before he answered. "It's best."

"Why?"

Sighing, he leaned back in his chair, looking directly at her. "Becca, I realize you want Folger to pay for what he did to your father, but a range war with Bonnie Blue men getting killed isn't the way to do it."

"I agree," she said, nodding, "but your going over there alone and getting killed doesn't sound like a very good plan, either."

"I don't figure on getting killed." He sat forward again and continued eating.

Do not yell, Becca told herself firmly. "Oh? And, pray tell, just how do you intend to keep that from happening, Mr. Ironbow?" she asked, just as sweetly as she could.

"Don't worry about it."

She pounded the table with her fist, sloshing the coffee in their cups into the saucers.

"Dammit," she exclaimed, "I *am* worried about it. I don't want you killed, or hurt, or anything. Can you understand that, Slade? I couldn't bear it if anything happened to you, because I . . . because . . ." She drew in an unsteady breath. "Because I just couldn't," she finished in a small voice.

Slade frowned as he looked at her. Her eyes were big and round, glistening with unshed tears. Her bottom lip trembled before she caught it with her teeth, and the color drained from her face. She looked frightened and vulnerable, as delicate as the china they were using.

She was truly afraid for him, he thought incredulously. He had never known any other woman to care that deeply about him, and he was filled with a foreign but pleasant sense of warmth.

"There's nothing to worry about, Becca," he said in a gentle voice. "It's a bluff, that's all. Folger won't believe I'm alone, not for a minute. This way, no one gets hurt."

"I see," she said slowly. "Folger will think that Bonnie Blue men are out there somewhere, ready to move in at your signal?"

He nodded.

"Well, I guess it's reasonable. Sort of. Thank you for explaining it to me, Slade."

"Yep," he said, redirecting his attention to his stew.

"I suppose you're not accustomed to being asked why you're going to do something," she said.

"No."

"Are you angry that I pressed you for answers?"

He hesitated a moment, then looked at her. "No. No, Becca, I'm not angry. I don't know why, but I'm not."

"Oh."

She smiled at him, a gentle, warm smile that set his heart racing and his blood running hot in his veins. He pushed his chair back and got to his feet. Becca did the same.

"No, finish your supper," he said. "Sit down."

"I've had enough."

"Dammit, Becca, sit down!"

She blinked. "Why is it suddenly so important that I sit down? You're not making any sense. When a person is finished with their supper they get up from the table and—"

The past days spent in controlling the ever growing awareness of her, the engulfing desire she inspired were taking a toll. He took one step around the end of the table, slid his hand to the nape of her neck, and brought his mouth down hard on hers.

He hadn't meant to kiss her. He'd told himself he wasn't going to kiss or touch her again, not ever. He would stop kissing her . . . later.

His other arm slid around her waist to pull her to him, and Becca went willingly as the kiss gentled and their tongues met. She was vaguely aware of a tug on the ribbon in her hair, then felt his hand weaving through the heavy tresses. She pressed against him, savoring his heat, his taste, his aroma. Savoring Slade.

He slowly lifted his head, his breathing rough. Filling his hands with her hair, he sifted it through his fingers and let it fall over her breasts.

"Beautiful," he murmured.

Becca didn't speak, not wishing to break the sensual spell that enveloped them. She was awash with desire, her breasts heavy and aching, and she knew that only Slade's touch would soothe the sweet pain. His kiss had been ecstasy, but she wanted more, so much more.

He drew his thumb lightly over her lips, then took a step backward, dropping his hands to his sides.

"I told you that wouldn't happen again," he said. "I didn't intend to kiss you. I . . . Ah, hell, I don't know." He raked a hand through his hair. "I don't understand half of what I do when I'm with you. I don't usually talk this much, either."

She smiled.

"Dammit," he yelled, "quit smiling at me like that!"

"Like what?" she asked, all innocence.

"Like a woman who knows some secret. That smile just got you kissed, lady, and unless you want to make love in the middle of this table, I suggest you stop smiling that smile right now!"

"Mercy, mercy, mercy," Maria said, bustling into the room. "If you're going to have a tumble on the table, let me clear away the good china. This came all the way from the East, and it's not easy to replace."

"Maria!" Becca exclaimed in shock.

"Now, personally," Maria went on, stacking the dishes, "I'm old-fashioned enough to think that lovemaking should be done in a soft feather bed." She paused. "Or maybe in sweet-smelling hay. Or—"

"Maria, don't you say another word," Becca interrupted, feeling the flush of embarrassment on her cheeks. "You can't talk about things like that. It just isn't proper."

"I'm just adding my opinion," Maria said. "Slade here was the one saying that this table would do just fine. To each his own, but I'll have my china out of the way first, if you please."

Becca covered her face with her hands. "This is mortifying."

Slade laughed, a rumbly laugh from deep in his chest. He gave Maria a loud kiss on the forehead, then strode from the room, still chuckling.

"Mercy," Maria said, smiling, "he's full of the devil, that one."

Becca sat down in her chair with a thud. "You were no help, Maria Sanchez," she said crossly. "Shame on you for the things you were saying about—about what you were saying things about."

Maria's smile grew bigger. "You look so pretty, Becca, with your cheeks flushed, your lips red from kissing, and your hair all tousled and hanging free."

"Hush." Becca snatched the ribbon from the floor and tried in vain to pull her hair back into a semblance of order. With a sigh she abandoned the effort, plunked her elbows on the table, and rested her chin on top of folded hands. "Oh, dear."

Maria looked at her for a long moment, then sat down in Slade's chair, her smile gone. "Becca, honey, don't be so upset. Talk to your old Maria and tell me what's in your heart. Tell me what you're thinking about Slade Ironbow."

"Oh, Maria, I'm so confused. I've never met anyone like him before. Not ever. He makes me feel . . . When he . . . I feel like . . ." Her voice trailed off.

"A woman?"

Becca looked at Maria. "Yes," she whispered, "a woman."

"It's time, you know, even overdue. Becca, Jed spoke to me of this more than once. He was concerned because he often felt he was being selfish, allowing you to be such a part of the Bonnie Blue when other girls were busy setting their cap for the young bucks sniffing around. Yet, he knew that none of them that came calling were man enough for you. They wouldn't be strong enough for you, or strong enough to run the Bonnie Blue. I told him the right man would come along when the time was right and he shouldn't fret about it."

"My father actually talked about it with you?"

Maria nodded. "He surely did. And I'll tell you this, Jed Colten would approve of Slade Ironbow. Slade is a man of honor, despite his wearing his gun like a gunslinger. Your father would love to see what's happening between you, fussin' and fumin' one minute, then kissing like there's no tomorrow the next."

"But, Maria, what *is* happening? It's all so confusing. I feel strange, changed, ever since Slade got here."

"And womanly."

"Yes. Maria, how can I be sure I've fallen in love with Slade?"

"Oh, honey, you'll know. There won't be any doubt in your mind, believe me."

"You're sure?"

"I'm sure."

Becca sighed again. "And what about Slade? What if he disappears just as quickly as he came? He's here to pay a debt to my father for someone else. What if he manages to stop Folger, then just . . . goes? Oh, Maria, what if he doesn't feel anything for me at all?"

"That man is feeling something, honey."

"Lust," Becca said, wrinkling her nose.

"No, it's more than lust. Why do you think he's sputtering mad half the time? Men like Slade aren't used to heart trouble, Becca. They pride themselves on their control of all situations at all times. Takes quite a woman to be their undoing, and they'll fight it every inch of the way. For a while. Loving a man like Slade wouldn't be easy, Becca, but then loving you would take a bushel of patience, too, my girl."

Becca straightened. "Well! That's not a very nice thing to say."

"It's true. Most young women act all helpless so as to make their fella feel manly. But you stand toe-to-toe with Slade, your temper flaring and your independence taking you where you want to go. But he's enough of a man within himself not to be scared off by you. The two of you together, it would never be dull or quiet around here, I'll tell you that."

"Oh, I don't like this one bit," Becca said, folding her arms over her breasts. "I don't know how I feel about Slade, and heavens knows I have no idea how he feels about me."

"But you do know how you feel when he takes you in his arms and kisses you."

"Oh, yes," she said wistfully. "It's wonderful. Exciting and frightening at the same time. There's a heat inside me. I want . . . That is . . . Just forget I said all that."

Maria laughed and stood up. "You're the one who can't forget it, and I'd bet Slade can't, either. Listen to your heart, Becca. You'll find your answers there."

Becca got to her feet. "Things were easier when I was a little girl."

"Being a woman is no small chore, honey. You're tired. Why don't you go to the bathing room and take a long hot soak. I'll help you heat the water and fill the tub, then you'll have a real good night's sleep."

"Yes, maybe I will. Oh, that's ridiculous. Slade is going to Folger's alone tonight. He caught the man who set trip wires that killed my father and hurt Frank. The man was to meet Folger at ten o'clock and Slade is going in his place. And he's going alone, the idiot."

"Slade knows what he's doing, Becca."

"I won't sleep a wink until he's back safely from Folger's. The thought of anything happening to him just gives me icy chills."

Maria smiled. "That's your heart speaking to you. You best learn to pay attention. You go on now and I'll be right along to help you with your bath."

"All right." She gave Maria a tight hug. "I love you. Thank you."

Maria watched Becca leave the room. "I'm doing my best for her, Mattie," she said softly.

In the bunkhouse Slade had joined Yancey and Frank. "Yancey filled me in," Frank said to him. "Hope you don't get yourself killed over at Folger's tonight, Slade."

Slade chuckled. "Wasn't planning on it." He pulled his chair closer to Frank's bunk. "Frank, I heard about a law being passed, that all cattle brands had to be registered with county officials to make them the legal property of a ranch. Has that law come this far West?"

"Sure has," Frank said. "Jed put the Bonnie Blue brand—back-to-back B's—on a leather swatch and sent me down to Houston to get it registered."

"When?"

" 'Bout a year ago now. You only have to do it every ten years, so we're fine."

"Do you know if Folger registered his brand?"

"No, I don't. If his pa was still alive you can be sure it was done. But Henry Folger? I can see him deciding it was just too much trouble, and also feeling he was above having to follow some fancy new law to protect his cattle."

"Is there a telegraph line into Jubele?" Slade asked.

"Yep. There's a nosy old biddy working the thing. If Brady Webster wants something kept private, he just shoos her out and sends the telegram himself."

"Good," Slade said. "Yancey, tomorrow you go into Jubele and have Webster telegraph to Houston. Find out if Folger registered his brand. Make sure no one but you and the sheriff knows you're checking."

"I'll go first thing," Yancey said. "Want me to tell Brady

anything about Gil and them trip wires you found out was used?"

"I'll let you know when I get back from Folger's tonight."

"Why you checking to see if Folger registered his brand?" Frank asked. "What are you up to, Slade?"

"Maybe something, maybe nothing." He stood up. "I'll look in on you later. Go easy on that leg . . . Frankie."

"Frankie?" Yancey repeated as Slade left.

"Oh, hell," Frank muttered.

Yancey leaned toward him. "Frankie?"

Frank sighed. "Might as well tell you, I suppose. See, I was in San Antonio, drunk as a skunk, and. . . ."

Ten

Just before ten o'clock that night, Slade swung out of the saddle and dropped his horse's reins to the ground. His gaze swept over the ranch house of Four Aces, clearly visible in the moonlight.

It was as big as the Colten house, but it had a shabby look to it. As he crossed the porch, warped boards creaked under him. He knocked on the door. It was opened immediately by the man he recognized as Casey, and lamplight poured over the two of them.

"What the hell are you doing here?" Casey exclaimed, his hand dropping to his gun.

"Gil couldn't make it," Slade said. "I want to see Folger."

Casey looked beyond Slade, his gaze darting back and forth as he squinted into the night. He glanced at Slade again, frowned, then spun on his heel and strode back down the hall.

"Stay there, Ironbow," he snapped over his shoulder.

Slade stepped into the hall and closed the door behind

him. A minute later, Casey leaned out of a room halfway down the hall.

"All right, come on," he said.

Slade walked down the hall, scanning the area. The house was richly furnished, but everything was covered by a layer of dust. The large room he entered was over-stuffed with furniture, its wood dull, the chair cushions stained. A huge fire roared in the hearth, making the room stifling hot.

Sitting in a high-backed leather chair close to the flames was a man dressed in dark pants and a burgundy velvet smoking jacket. He was holding a brandy snifter in one hand, and his gaze was trained on Slade.

Slade stopped in the middle of the room, studying his adversary. A soft belly strained against the velvet jacket, and a silk cravat couldn't hide Folger's double chin. The flush on his puffy cheeks and his red nose and eyes indicated Folger was a heavy drinker. Slade knew he was in his middle thirties, but he looked ten years older, his thinning brown hair plastered down on his balding head.

"Folger," he said, nodding slightly.

Folger's gaze slid contemptuously over Slade. "Well, well, well," he said, his speech slightly thick with drink, "the Injun has come calling. The great Slade Ironbow. To what do I owe this dubious honor?"

"Just thought I'd let you know that Gil is, shall we say, tied up." Slade walked over to a bar next to the fireplace and poured himself a drink.

"Hey," Casey said. "Mr. Folger didn't offer you nothin'."

"Oh, let the Injun have some firewater," Folger said. "So, Ironbow, you're a bold man walking in here alone. I suppose I'm to believe there are no Bonnie Blue men outside waiting for your signal to move in?"

Slade shrugged and took a sip of liquor. "Believe what you want."

"I'm not a fool. I know they're out there. Just what is it you want here?"

"Not much," Slade said. "This is simply a neighborly call. Isolated ranches like these should keep each other up-to-date on the recent news."

"Oh, how nice." Folger drained his glass, then held it in the air. Casey hurried to refill it from the bottle sitting on a table by Folger's elbow. "Do give me your neighborly news, Ironbow."

Slade casually rested one forearm on the dusty surface of the wood bar. "News is, Folger," he said, looking directly at the man, "that you hired Gil to set trip wires that killed Jed Colten and broke Frank Tatum's leg."

Folger stiffened for an instant, then relaxed again, a smirk on his face.

"Interesting," he said. "You have proof of this wild accusation?"

"I have Gil."

Folger laughed, a high-pitched, eerie sound. Casey shifted nervously, glancing between Folger and Slade.

"Of course," Folger said, a wicked smile on his florid face, "I don't know anyone named Gil. He's probably a drifter, I imagine, making up stories to save his own hide. I'm an important man in these parts, Ironbow. You take this footloose cowboy's word against mine?"

Slade stared Folger down.

"Why you wasting my time?" Folger said.

"Just sharing news."

"Do go on then," Folger said, waving his glass at Slade. "This is entertaining. Indians are known for puttin' on fascinatin' shows."

Casey swallowed heavily. "Mr. Folger, maybe you shouldn't be getting Ironbow all riled up about him being a—"

"Shut up, Casey," Folger said fiercely. "This is my home. If I allow a half-breed into it, I'll speak to him any way I choose."

"Fine," Casey said quickly. He shot Slade another nervous glance.

"Go on with your . . . news," Folger said.

"Well, the news is, Folger," Slade said, straightening and hooking his thumbs in his gun belt, "that I know you're a murderer. News is that one of your men took a shot at me and Becca Colten. News is that you'll never have the Bonnie Blue. And the news is that if you or any of your men come near Becca Colten or Bonnie Blue land again, I'm going to kill you and them." He nodded. "That about brings you right up to the minute."

Folger slammed his snifter onto the table with such force, the glass shattered. Liquor sprayed in all directions, staining Folger's pants and velvet jacket. The air was heavy with the odor of brandy.

"Don't threaten me," Folger said through clenched teeth. "No one threatens Henry Folger. The Bonnie Blue will be mine, Indian, and so will the lovely Becca. Oh, I do look forward to the day—and the night—that she becomes my wife. She'll have no choice but to marry me to save her precious land; then that land will be mine. I courted her proper, asked her to marry me, but she turned me down. Now, we're doing this my way. I won't be stopped. Your arrival on the Bonnie Blue was a bit of a surprise, but nothing I can't handle. I killed Jed Colten, and I'll kill you."

"Mr. Folger," Casey said, "you shouldn't be saying that you—"

"Casey, not another word!" Folger yelled. "Who's going to believe this half-breed's word against mine? No one. No one will believe Gil, either. Accidents happen on ranches. That's the way it is. I can't be stopped. The enticing Miss Colten will tire of it all soon enough. She'll be only too happy to marry me and merge the two ranches. And I'll be only too happy to have Becca Colten in my bed. I'm looking forward to that. Oh, yes, I certainly am."

Every muscle in Slade's body tensed, and he forced himself to continue giving the appearance of being relaxed and calm. The image of Folger touching Becca tightened the knot of rage, sending the blood pounding through his veins.

"And that, Ironbow," Folger said, "is *my* neighborly news. It's time for you to leave my home."

Slade started across the room. "Just remember what I said, Folger. You and your men stay away from Becca Colten and the Bonnie Blue. If you don't, you'll be dead."

Folger attempted to lunge out of the chair, but his hands slipped on the arms and he sank back heavily.

"I told you not to threaten me, Indian. You're fast with that gun. I've heard of you, your reputation. But you're one man. Your Bonnie Blue cowboys can pull a trigger, but I have trained gunmen here. Numbers, Ironbow. That's what's important, and I have you cold. One fast-on-the-draw half-breed isn't going to be enough to save the Bonnie Blue, or Becca Colten."

Slade walked out the door.

"Do you hear me, Ironbow?" Folger yelled after him. "The Bonnie Blue will be mine. Becca will be mine. Mine!"

Slade left the house without closing the door behind him, and moments later was galloping away from Four Aces. His jaw was clenched so tightly his teeth ached, and he slowed his horse, forcing himself to relax and cool his fury.

By the time he reached the Bonnie Blue, he was once more in control. He rode straight to the bunkhouse, where he found Yancey playing cards with Frank. The sound of men snoring echoed in the building.

"Welcome back," Yancey said, "You look mad as hell."

Slade hunkered down by the bed and shoved his Stetson back. "Folger has pickled his brain with liquor," he said quietly. "He's sick, which makes him even more dangerous."

"And his men?" Frank asked.

"If Casey is any indication, Folger is paying them enough to do as he says. They're gunfighters, not cowhands, and that could work in our favor. Yancey, I'll go into Jubele tomorrow instead of you. I think it's time to bring Brady Webster up-to-date. There are a couple of other telegrams I need to send too. I'll take Becca with me."

Yancey nodded. "What about Gil?"

"Folger is denying he knows Gil, which is what we figured. I'll talk to Webster and see if there's somewhere we can stash Gil. I'm not having Bonnie Blue men losing sleep guarding him, but Folger would find a way to kill him if he's sitting in a jail cell."

"You're covering all the corners, Slade," Frank said.

"So far, anyway. Problem is, I can't think like Folger, can't even guess what he might do next. He's like a crazy man on the subject of having this ranch and"—his jaw tightened—"and Becca."

"We've got to stop him," Yancey said.

Slade pushed himself to his feet and tugged his Stetson low on his forehead. When he spoke, his voice was as cold as the winter wind. "I told Folger that if he didn't stay away from Becca and the Bonnie Blue, I'd kill him. I made it clear that included his men too. Nothing, gentlemen, is going to happen to Becca Colten." He turned and strode from the room.

Becca threw back the blankets and slipped from her bed. She was unable to tolerate one more moment of straining to hear any sound that would mean Slade had returned safely from Four Aces.

Pulling on a lightweight white wrapper over her white cotton nightgown, she walked to the wall that connected her room with Slade's. Pressing her ear against it, she listened hard, then sighed.

This was ridiculous, she thought, straightening and

planting her hands on her hips. Slade was part Indian and moved with smooth litheness. *Quiet,* smooth litheness. For all she knew, he was long since back and sleeping like a baby in his bed, while she tortured herself with images of what might be happening to him.

She scowled. If Slade Ironbow was asleep in the other room she was going to wake him up and punch him in the nose! How dare he put her through this. Her mind had conjured up horrible, frightening pictures of a confrontation between Slade and Folger, and all those gunfighters that Folger had hired, and . . .

Becca pressed her hands to her cheeks. Dear heaven, she thought frantically, what if Slade was hurt? What if Folger was holding him captive at Four Aces? No, oh, please, no. Slade was all right, he had to be. Because she loved him.

She crossed the room on trembling legs and sank onto her bed. Maria had told her to listen to the voice of her heart, and her heart was singing the song of love.

An intoxicating joy filled her. *Becca Colten was in love with Slade Ironbow.*

It was glorious. And frightening. Wonderful. And terrifying.

"I love Slade, Pa," she whispered to the night, "but I don't know what to do about it. I really don't."

She frowned. What she was going to do at that very moment, she decided, was check Slade's room.

She stood, tightened the sash on her wrapper, and walked to the door. Her eyes had long since become accustomed to the darkness, and she could complete her mission without lighting a lamp. As she opened her door and stepped into the hall, she told herself there was no reason to feel like a thief in her own house. She was simply going to peek into Slade's room to see if he was asleep there.

She padded down the hall in her bare feet, the wild

pounding of her heart echoing in her ears. At Slade's door, she reached out a trembling hand, hesitated, then gripped the doorknob and turned it slowly. As she pushed the door open, she remembered, finally, to breathe. Releasing her tight grip on the doorknob, she tiptoed to the foot of the double bed.

Empty.

"Oh, God," she whispered. Slade wasn't back from Four Aces! Why not? What was taking so long? What was happening to him at that ranch? Why wasn't Slade home?

"Was there something you wanted?" a deep voice asked.

Eleven

Becca gasped and spun around.

Standing tall and massive just inside the room was Slade. Before she'd even realized she'd moved, she ran across the room and flung herself at him, wrapping her arms around his neck and burying her face in the crook of his neck. Slade staggered slightly from the unexpected impact, then embraced her, lifting her feet from the floor.

"I was so worried about you," she said, her words muffled against his shirt collar. "I couldn't stand it another minute, so I came in here to see if you'd returned and I hadn't heard you. Oh, thank God, you're all right. I'm so glad you're safe, Slade. So glad you're home."

Slade had been momentarily stunned by Becca's flinging herself against him, but now he was very aware that he was holding her tightly to him. He filled his senses with her delicate aroma, with the feel of her soft body pressed to his hard one. Her words echoed in his mind.

Home.

His arms tightened around her as he lowered his head, burying his face in her silken hair. Her breasts were crushed to his chest, the thin material of her gown and wrapper little barrier between them. His body hardened with desire.

Home, he repeated silently. Yes, he was home.

Becca suddenly realized where she was and what she had done. She stiffened in Slade's arms, a flush of embarrassment staining her cheeks as she slowly lifted her head.

"Oh, dear," she said breathlessly. "I didn't mean to . . . That is, I . . ." She met his gaze. "I think it would be best if you put me down."

"No."

"No? Don't be silly. We can't stand here like this all night. Besides, your gun belt is poking me."

"Well, then I guess I *will* have to put you down."

He slid her slowly, sensuously along his body, his gaze never leaving hers. She gasped when she felt his arousal. Her feet finally touched the floor and she flattened her hands on his chest. His hands slid beneath her hair to rest on her shoulders.

"Did you feel what you do to me?" he asked, his voice husky.

"Yes," she whispered.

"Becca," he murmured; then his mouth claimed hers.

All thought fled as heat coiled and pulsed, deep within Becca. She met his tongue with hers, leaning into him, feeling again his heavy arousal. She wanted him, ached for him with a burning hunger she knew only he could appease.

His hands roamed down her back and over her buttocks to nestle her into the cradle of his hips. He tore his lips from hers, then trailed a ribbon of kisses down the side of her slender neck. She tipped her head back, her eyes closed, and he kissed the wildly beating pulse at the base of her throat.

"I want you," he murmured. "I want to make love to you."

"Yes. Oh, yes, I want you, too."

His lips found hers again in a searing kiss as he undid the sash at her waist. He pushed the wrapper from her shoulders, and she let it fall to the floor.

The curtains on the window were open, and silvery moonlight poured over her as she stood before him. Passion roared through Slade as he saw all that she was outlined beneath the thin cotton nightgown. Her breasts were full, waiting for his hands, his mouth, to caress them. Her small waist, curving hips, and long legs beckoned to him.

She opened her eyes and met his gaze. He saw no fear there, no trepidation. He saw woman, his woman, desire clouding her eyes and a soft smile touching her lips. He lifted one hand and drew his thumb over her kiss-swollen lips. She closed her eyes, and he knew she wouldn't refuse him.

Without speaking, he turned and quietly closed and locked the door. He threw his Stetson onto a chair, then took off his shirt. The gun belt was set on the dresser, then he sat on the bed and pulled off his boots. He could feel Becca's gaze on him, and his desire flared even higher. Standing again, he tossed back the blankets and looked at her. He paused, holding her gaze, then undid his belt. Moments later he stood naked before her in the shower of moonlight that flowed through the window.

"Oh, Slade," she whispered, her voice filled with awe.

He extended one hand to her and waited. Her gaze swept over his tightly muscled body. Dark hair covered the bronzed skin of his chest. His legs were powerful, his hips lean, and his manhood . . . Heat flooded through her. His manhood boldly proclaimed his desire for her.

Her heart singing with joy, she pushed the narrow straps of her gown down her arms. The gown slid from her heated body, pooling at her feet.

She stepped free and walked to Slade.

Her gaze never wavering, she lifted one hand and placed it in his. His fingers closed around hers, and she looked at their entwined hands for a moment before meeting his smoldering gaze again.

"You are home," she said softly, "and I am home."

Nameless emotions churned within Slade, and he welcomed them, along with the warmth and peace they brought to his soul. He gathered her close and held her for a long moment as though she were made of delicate china.

"You," he said finally, his voice hoarse with passion, "are the most beautiful woman I've ever seen."

"And you," she answered, "are magnificent."

"Are you frightened, Becca?"

"No, not of you. My only fear is that I won't know how to please you."

"You please me by just being you." He paused. "Becca, are you sure this is what you want? I can still stop if—"

"Make love to me, Slade. I want you so much." *And I love you so much. I will love you forever, Slade Ironbow.* "Please?"

He swung her up into his arms and kissed her, his tongue plummeting into her mouth. She met his tongue with her own, returning the kiss with an ardor that spoke of her increasing desire. He laid her on the cool sheets, then paused for a moment to gaze at her before stretching out next to her. He kissed her again, a soft, sensuous kiss, as his hand stroked across her flat stomach. Then his hand inched upward to her breasts, hesitating before cupping one. His thumb stroked the taut nipple.

"Oh, my," Becca gasped. "Slade."

He dipped his head to draw that nipple deep into his mouth, sucking it, laving it with his tongue. Becca's eyes drifted closed in pure pleasure. His rhythmic sucking was matched by a pulsing deep within her. When Slade moved to her other breast, heat swept through her entire body, setting her on fire. She sank her hands into his thick dark hair and pressed his mouth harder onto her, offering more, wanting more. She could feel his arousal heavy against her hip, and gloried in the knowledge that they had just begun their journey together, with so much more to come.

He lifted his head, and she instantly missed the feel of his mouth on her breast. His hand skimmed over the curve of her hip, then trailed inward to the part of her known—but not really known—only to herself.

"Trust me," he murmured.

"Yes."

His fingers found her moist heat, her most secret place, and she stiffened, her eyes questioning.

"Trust me," he repeated.

"I . . . Oh . . ."

She sighed, relaxing again as sensations she'd never known before consumed her. Slade's fingers were instruments of sweet torture, his lips never still as they caressed her. She arched her back and whispered his name as pressure built within her. Deep, so deep and new, strange and wondrous. Pleasure heightened within her, and she clutched his shoulders.

"Slade, please . . . I feel . . . I need . . ." she choked out. "I don't know. Slade . . ."

"Trust me," he said once more, then moved over her, catching his weight on his forearms. And she did trust him, he realized. She was giving him the gift of her innocence, and he had to make this perfect for her. But she felt so small, so delicate beneath him. What if he hurt her? He was at the edge of his control, his entire body aching from restraint. But he had to go carefully.

He kissed her, then parted her legs and entered the sweet haven of her femininity. Slowly, his muscles quivering from tension, he slipped into her until nature's barrier stopped him.

"Hold on to me, Becca," he said, his breathing rough. "There will be pain, but it won't last, and then I promise you it will be wonderful."

He gritted his teeth and surged into her, catching her sharp cry with his mouth. Gathering every ounce of his willpower, he waited until he felt her relax again.

"Now, my Becca," he whispered, "now we'll ride with the wind. Together."

"Together," she echoed.

Gently at first, Slade drove deeper and deeper within her. Becca matched his rhythm instinctively, taking all that he offered, giving all that she was. He slid one arm beneath her hips to lift her to him as the cadence quickened. Pounding, thundering, like a mighty stallion chasing the wind. Ecstasy. Heat. Sensations twisting within Becca, a tempestuous storm gathering force. She strained upward, seeking, yet not knowing what she sought . . . until suddenly she was hurled into the wind, splintered into a million brightly colored pieces. Slade thrust one last time, then shuddered as he joined her, his seed spilling into her, his strength passing from him to her.

He collapsed against her, then found the strength to roll onto his back, taking her with him, their bodies still meshed. He wrapped his arms tightly around her as she nestled her head on his moist chest. Neither spoke as their breathing quieted.

Never, Slade thought hazily, had he experienced a joining such as this. It had been far beyond the usual physical release he sought to satisfy his bodily hunger.

With Becca, the basic need had intertwined with new emotions that touched his soul, his heart.

He tightened his hold on her, thinking fleetingly that he would never let her go. She was truly his now.

"Becca?" he asked quietly. "Are you all right?"

"I never knew it would be so beautiful," she whispered.

"It was beautiful because you gave all of yourself to me."

And she'd done that because she loved him, she thought. How she yearned to tell him of her love, but she knew this wasn't the time. Slade wasn't ready to hear those words. And she was too fragile to bear the weight of his silence if he didn't return those words. She would simply cherish this moment and the splendor of what they had shared.

Slade eased her off him and tucked her close to his side, then pulled the blankets over them.

"Sleep," he murmured, sifting his fingers through her hair. "It's very late. We're going into Jubele in the morning."

"Why?"

"Just sleep now. I'll explain it all later."

"What happened at Folger's?"

"Later, Becca."

She yawned. "All right. I feel so . . . I don't know. So peaceful, contented, as though we're the only two people in the world. There's nothing beyond that door. No problems, no dangers, just us, here, together. I'm . . . so . . . sleepy."

He kissed her on the forehead. "Good night, Becca."

"Mmm," she said. Then her breathing slowed as she drifted off to sleep.

Slade held her close, staring up into the darkness. He was, he knew, going to have to look deep within himself to discern what emotions were churning there. And he'd have to face the ramifications of taking the precious gift of Becca's innocence.

But not tonight.

Tonight belonged to him and Becca, to the silvery moonlight and the wind. With the dawn would come reality, but he would not allow it to intrude on this night.

He closed his eyes, and with Becca held safely within the circle of his arms, he slept.

Twelve

Becca stirred, opening her eyes to see bright sunlight filling the room. Why wasn't she in her own bed? she wondered foggily. As the haze of sleep lifted, the events of the previous night rushed in on her. She turned her head to stare at the empty expanse of bed next to her.

Where was Slade? And why was the room so bright with sunlight? Not difficult questions, she thought dryly, if a person was halfway alert. Slade had risen early, and she'd slept well past her usual waking hour of dawn.

Slade, she mused, stretching leisurely. Slade Ironbow. Heavens, she even savored the very sound of his name. Oh, how she loved him. And how glorious their lovemaking had been, more beautiful than her most secret fantasies and dreams.

She had no regrets, she realized. She felt no shame or guilt. There were many who would call her a whore for lying with a man without benefit of marriage, but she knew the depth of her love for Slade, knew she was committed to him for all time, as though she'd spoken vows in front of a preacher.

But what of Slade? What of his feelings for her? He cared for her, she was sure of it. She would have to be patient, give him time to listen to the voice of his heart. Oh, yes, she would wait for Slade.

Smiling, Becca threw back the blankets and sat up. She gasped as she felt a soreness in the private places of her body, then quickly donned her nightgown and wrapper.

She opened the bedroom door and stepped into the hall at the same moment that Maria came out of her room. They stopped, their eyes meeting.

"I came to wake you," Maria said. "Slade said the two of you are going into Jubele, and it's time you were getting ready."

"Yes, we're going into town." Becca walked down the hall. "I . . . You know, don't you?"

"Becca, you came out of Slade's room, and you have the glow that says you just woke up. I think that if I checked Slade's bed, I'd find the evidence of your lost innocence."

"Oh." She flushed. "That."

"Yes, that. Nature's gift that is yours to give to the man you love. Come into your room, Becca, so we can talk."

Becca lifted her chin and went into the bedroom. Maria followed and closed the door.

"Becca—" Maria began.

"No," Becca said, raising one hand for silence. "Let me have my say first. I love you as though you were my mother, and if you really were my mother, or if my father were standing here right now, I'd be saying these exact same words. I love Slade Ironbow with every breath in my body. I'm not ashamed or sorry that I made love with him. I listened to the voice of my heart and I knew I loved him. I'll never believe that what Slade and I did was wrong." She halted her rush of words as she ran out of air, and took a deep breath.

"Are you finished?" Maria asked.

"Well, I guess so. There doesn't seem to be anything else to say."

"Then I'll go change the linens on Slade's bed while you wash and dress. I kept some breakfast warm for you."

"Maria, how can you stand there talking about breakfast? I have just made love with a man without benefit of marriage. You're like a mother to me, Maria. Aren't you supposed to yell, or cry, or tell me I'm a wanton woman, or . . . something?"

Maria laughed softly. "Come sit with me for a minute, honey." She sat on the edge of the bed, then patted the place next to her. "Come on."

Becca did as instructed, folding her hands tightly in her lap as she looked at Maria.

"I promised your mother," Maria began, "that I'd do my best in helping to raise you. Not everyone feels the same about things, and we all have to hold true to our own beliefs. Most folks would say that what you and Slade did was sinful. Becca, I learned a long time ago that we have to grab hold of happiness when it crosses our path. There are no guarantees in this life; things just don't always go as we planned."

Becca nodded.

"I look at you now," Maria went on, "and I see a glow of happiness in your eyes. How can I judge what you did as wrong? I can't. You're a woman in love. I don't know what the future will bring you, but at this moment you're filled with a wondrous joy that some women never know. Cherish it, protect it; it is a precious treasure. Love Slade with all that you are, and worry about the tomorrows when they get here."

Becca's eyes brimmed with tears and she flung her arms around Maria's neck. "Oh, Maria, I love you. Thank you. Thank you so much."

"Now then," Maria said, blinking back her own tears,

"you get ready to go to town. Slade asked me if you wore those pants of yours into Jubele, and I said you always put on a dress. He'll be bringing the buggy around soon."

"Yes, I'll hurry," Becca said, dashing the tears from her cheeks.

"I said this to you after your pa's funeral," Maria added, "and I'm saying it again: Jed wouldn't want you in mourning clothes. He didn't believe in it. He grieved deeply for his Bonnie, but he saw to it that this house was filled with sunshine and laughter. Don't worry about what folks in Jubele will say—you wear a pretty dress for Slade. Your pa would have wanted you to."

"All right."

Maria got to her feet. "You get a move on now. We can talk about this again later, if you like. I'll always be here for you, honey." She left the room and closed the door behind her."

"Thank you, Maria," Becca whispered.

Slade strode toward the barn to ready the buggy for the ten-mile trip to Jubele. Conflicting emotions warred within him. The contentment of having made love with Becca battled with the sharp need to have her again. His satisfaction at having made her his struggled with his long-held belief that no woman would ever claim him. The only emotion missing was guilt.

Instead of feeling guilt at taking Becca's innocence, he felt a rightness at their joining. And that angered him. What had she done to him to so thoroughly shake up his self-control, to make him question the safe structure of his life?

He hitched the horse to the buggy and led it around the corner of the house, nurturing his anger, allowing it to grow. It was an emotion with a name, one he understood. Yes, anger would do just fine.

He slid his rifle into the brackets beneath the seat of the buggy, then tied the horse's reins loosely around one of the porch pillars. His jaw set in a tight line, he bounded up the steps of the porch and leaned his shoulder against a pillar, his arms crossed over his chest. He stared at the front door, through which the source of his unrest and agitation would come in the form of Miss Becca Colten.

And then, there she was.

In a simple dress the color of daffodils, her auburn hair caught at the nape of her neck with a matching yellow ribbon, Becca stepped out onto the porch.

"Hello, Slade," she said softly, and smiled.

The sudden, wild beating of Slade's heart echoed in his ears like the throbbing of Indian drums. His breath quickened and heat flared within him.

The anger he had struggled to maintain quickly dissipated as passion rushed through him, intertwined with the now-familiar warmth that touched his heart, soul, and mind.

Before he realized he was moving, he straightened and shoved his Stetson back. His dark gaze linked with hers, and he started toward her as though he were being pulled by invisible strings.

Becca was pinned in place by Slade's mesmerizing eyes. The smooth, lithe power of his body evoked images of a sleek mountain lion. And then she remembered that magnificent body naked, bronzed, moving over her to join them in one entity of wondrous ecstasy.

Despite her trembling knees, she lifted her chin and held his gaze steadily. He stopped only inches from her, then slowly lifted his large hands to frame her face. His eyes traced her features one by one, lingering on her lips.

"Are you all right?" he asked.

"Yes, I'm fine," she said, a thread of breathlessness in her voice. "In body and mind, I'm fine, Slade."

He nodded. "Good. You look very pretty in that dress, like a spring flower."

"The people in Jubele may disapprove of my not wearing mourning clothes, but my father had strong feelings about that. Maria reminded me that Pa wouldn't have wanted me in black."

"The more I hear about Jed Colten, the more I realize I would have liked and respected him." He stroked her soft cheeks with his callused thumbs. "Just as I do his daughter."

"Oh, Slade," she whispered.

He lowered his head, and his mouth captured hers. He parted her lips, drinking of her sweetness as a bee suckles on the nectar from a flower.

A soft purr of pleasure escaped Becca's lips, causing a groan of need to catch in Slade's throat. He pulled himself from the passionate haze and lifted his head, drawing a rough breath. He stepped back and stared at a spot somewhere above Becca's left shoulder.

"It's time to get to Jubele," he said gruffly.

He spun on his heel and strode down the steps, flipping the reins free of the pillar without breaking stride.

Becca blinked, then took a breath and wondered if her shaking legs would carry her to the buggy. As she followed him, she watched the fascinating play of the muscles in Slade's back as he adjusted the reins on the patient horse.

Had she imagined it, she wondered. Or had Slade switched moods from gentle, warm, and wanting her, to abrupt and surly? Was he simply eager to get to Jubele, or had he had sudden second thoughts about kissing her? Was he regretting their beautiful lovemaking?

"Becca? Come on. It's getting late," he said, glancing at her over his shoulder.

She nodded and hurried down the steps. He assisted her onto the padded spring seat, but didn't look directly at her. A moment later he'd settled next to her, picked up the reins, and spoken in a low voice to the horse, tugging on the reins to turn the animal.

They left the Bonnie Blue accompanied by the sounds of birds singing and the steady rhythm of the horse's hooves. No words were spoken.

After several minutes of quiet Becca slid a glance at Slade. She might as well be sitting next to a tree trunk, she thought dismally, noting the tight set of his shoulders and jaw. A solid, unmoving tree trunk. Darn it, there was no keeping up with the man's mercurial mood changes. Well, she had no intention of sitting there in obedient silence during the entire trip to town. Slade Ironbow was going to talk to her.

She turned her head to look directly at his stony profile. "What happened at Folger's last night?"

"Not much," he said, continuing to stare straight ahead.

Patience, Becca told herself. "Would you care to elaborate on that a bit more?"

"No."

"Please?" Her voice rang with forced sweetness.

Slade lifted one shoulder in a shrug. "There's not a lot to tell. Folger is crazy from liquor, which makes him even more dangerous."

"He—he killed my father, didn't he?"

He nodded. "Yes. And he hired Gil to set the trip wires. Folger admitted having your father killed, Becca. He thinks he can't be touched because he's a big name around here, and Gil is a drifter."

"I see. Can you stop him, Slade?"

"Yes."

"Do you know how you're going to do it?"

"No."

"Dammit, Slade Ironbow," she yelled, "I really hate having conversations like this. Jed Colten was my father, remember? That snake in the grass Folger killed a wonderful, dear, loving man, and I have the right to know what your plans are for making Folger pay for what he did. I won't be pacified with your maddening 'yes' and 'no' answers. Talk to me."

Slade pushed his Stetson back and looked at her. "How can someone who looks like a spring flower sound like a cowboy? You really should curb your tongue, Miss Colten."

"That does it!" she exclaimed. She made a fist, pulled back her arm, and socked him on the shoulder as hard as she could. "Ow! You hurt my hand!"

"Me! You're the one getting violent." He chuckled. "Lord, you're something. A real hellcat." He shook his head and grinned at her. "Maybe Jed Colten should have planted his palm firmly on your backside a few times while you were growing up. You turned out to be a real handful, Becca Colten."

She sniffed indignantly, but couldn't hide her smile. "I only swear when my patience has been pushed beyond reasonable limits, sir, which is something you're very proficient at doing."

He chuckled again, then flicked the reins against the horse's back to increase the animal's speed. His smile faded as he scanned the area around them. Tall oak trees lined the dirt road for long stretches, followed by open expanses of desert that gave a clear view in every direction, all the way to the horizon.

He had to stay alert, he knew, for any sign of trouble. How closely Folger was having him watched, he didn't know. There was no denying that Becca was in danger by going into Jubele with him in an open buggy, but he wouldn't have drawn an easy breath the entire time he was in town if he'd left her behind on the Bonnie Blue.

"Slade?" Becca said, bringing him from his reverie. "Why are we going to Jubele today?"

"I want to talk to Brady Webster, tell him about Gil and what we know about the trip wires. I need to send some telegrams too."

"Telegrams?"

"I'll let you know if there's anything worth telling you, Becca. I'm following up on an idea that might not pan out. There's no use talking about it now."

She laughed. "That has a familiar ring to it. You obviously have an aversion to unnecessary, lengthy conversations. In fact, you have an aversion to lengthy conversations of any sort. I'm beginning to piece together the puzzle that is you, Slade Ironbow, a little bit at a time." She nodded decisively. "Yes, given time, I do believe I'll come to understand you, even though you're a very complicated man."

Slade frowned at her for a moment, then redirected his attention to the road. Complicated man? Him? And Becca was beginning to understand him? Good Lord, what did she possess, a secret path to his soul, the ability to see his hopes and dreams? Is that what it meant when a woman truly understood a man?

Hell, he fumed, he didn't know, because he'd never cared about a woman like this before.

He forced his jumbled thoughts under control and scanned the horizon.

Becca faced front again, swallowing a sigh at his silence. Minutes ticked by as the horse trotted steadily on to Jubele.

"Slade," Becca said finally, "would you mind telling me about your mother? You said you didn't know her very well before she died and . . . If you'd rather not discuss it, that's fine. I don't mean to pry."

"It was a long time ago, Becca."

"I know, but . . . No, I'm sorry. Forget that I asked."

He looked over at her for a long moment, then resumed his perusal of the countryside.

"My mother," he said, "was the daughter of missionaries who came to the Indian country. The fever struck one winter and her parents died. My mother was taken into my father's camp and made welcome. She was a young girl, maybe ten or eleven. She and my father became friends, then later it grew into more. When he was seventeen he took her as his wife. She was sixteen. A year passed and I was born, but my mother nearly died giving birth to me. She never regained her strength. My father knew she couldn't survive another harsh winter in the camp, and because he loved her as much as he did, he sent her back East to live with some distant relatives of hers. He never saw her again."

"He didn't visit her?"

"No. My father wouldn't walk in the white man's world back then. He was too proud, refused to leave his land. He sent me to her for several weeks each year, and she showed me white man's manners, dressed me in white man's clothes, taught me to read and write. When I was twelve, she died."

"Oh, Slade, I'm so sorry." She placed one hand on his arm, then drew it away as she felt his heat suffuse her. "I shouldn't have broached the subject and brought up what must be painful memories for you. I really do apologize."

"There's no need to apologize, Becca. Like I said, it was a long time ago. I can't clearly see my mother's face in my mind anymore. I remember that she had a soft, soothing voice, and that she always smelled like lilacs. What I learned from those visits to the East, though, was the fact that I wanted, and intended to have, what my heritage offered me. The Indian world and the white man's."

"And you've done that."

He nodded.

"I think that's wonderful, Slade."

"It has its drawbacks at times. You sure do get me talking, Becca. I've used up more than a few years of conversation since I met you. I'm not one to go on and on. There's just something about you . . . That must be Jubele up ahead there."

"Yes. It's not fancy, but it's growing all the time as people move West." She paused. "Slade, I'm flattered that you feel you can talk so openly with me."

"I sure as hell don't know why I do it," he said gruffly.

Maybe, Becca thought hopefully, it was because, without even realizing it, Slade was beginning to listen to the voice of his heart. She knew she shouldn't push him; she had to be patient and wait.

"Becca," he said, "you're to stay with me every minute we're in Jubele. We'll see the sheriff first and get him to clear the busybody out of the telegraph office. Whatever you hear is not to be repeated at the Bonnie Blue. I'll decide who is to know what."

"I can't even tell Maria?"

"No. I trust Maria, but what she doesn't know she can't slip up and say. If you have some shopping to do, I'll go with you once we've finished our business with Brady Webster. Understand?"

"I'll be right by your side, Slade. And you can trust me to keep still about what I hear, too."

"I know. I do trust you, Becca."

How deep did that trust run? he wondered. Was it the trust that caused him to reveal more of himself to Becca, more than he'd ever shown anyone else?

More damn questions, he thought. When this business with Folger was settled, when Becca and the Bonnie Blue were safe from harm, he was going to find the answers.

All of them.

Thirteen

The citizens of Dodge City were, without having been aware of it, eager for a change in their lives, a break in routines that varied little from one week to the next.

The news that Doc Willis was officially courting Mattie Muldoon spread like wildfire, and excitement crackled through the air. Soon the town was divided into two camps—those who were cheering on Doc Willis, and those who looked down their noses with righteous indignation.

Bartenders in every saloon were holding ever-increasing sums of money bet on the outcome of the courtship. The fact that Mattie had not yet accepted Doc's proposal of marriage was common knowledge, but odds were running high that she would, indeed, say yes to the persistent doctor.

Not even the most besotted, liquored-up cowboy, however, was willing to wager his hard-earned money on what would happen when Slade Ironbow returned to

Dodge. Everyone said Slade would call Doc out and shoot him deader than a doornail.

Late one afternoon, Abe knocked on Mattie's office door. She'd been pacing, distressed by the love letter Doc had sent her that morning, and angrily yanked the door open.

"Please, not another letter, Abe," she said helplessly.

"No, ma'am, a telegram," the big man said, handing her a yellow envelope. "Don't say much, though. Course, Slade never does run on with words."

Mattie narrowed her eyes. "You read my telegram, Abraham?"

"I wouldn't do no such thing, Mattie. Telegrams are private. The boy that brung it from the telegraph office told me what it said. I reckon the whole town will know in a bit that you heard from Slade and what he had to say. Not that he said much, of course, but I don't recall him ever sending you no telegram before when he was away. Why do you suppose he done that, Mattie?"

"Abe, you are a busybody," she said stiffly. "You outshine the Widow Sullivan in that department."

Abe roared with laughter, the booming sound echoing through the entire saloon.

Mattie shook her head and closed the office door. Quickly tearing open the envelope, she pulled the telegram out.

" 'Don't worry,' " she read aloud. " 'Should be over soon. Slade.' "

She squeezed her eyes closed for a moment, then silently read the words again as she walked into her inner room. Sinking into the leather chair Slade always sat in, she clutched the yellow paper to her breasts.

Slade was doing it. He was protecting her daughter and setting things to rights on the Bonnie Blue. Whatever trouble he had encountered with Henry Folger, he was bringing it under control, eliminating the danger.

"Oh, thank God," she whispered. It wasn't over yet, but "soon" Slade had said. "Soon."

She leaned back in the chair with a grateful sigh and closed her eyes again, giving way to the exhaustion that swept through her. She hadn't been sleeping well due to her concern for Slade and Becca, and her never-ending worry about Jim Willis and the price he would pay for his foolish courting of her.

The hazy mist of sleep crept over her, and she did not struggle against it. At least Becca was in safe hands, she thought. What was she like, her daughter, who'd been hers for only a fleeting moment? How were Becca and Slade getting on? What did they think of each other?

Slade and Becca. Becca . . . and Slade. How glorious . . . it would be . . . if they . . . fell . . . in love.

Mattie gave in to her weariness and slept.

Jubele, Texas, boasted just under twenty businesses housed in wooden buildings lining a wide, dusty street. Wooden sidewalks fronted the structures, along with hitching posts.

Slade pulled the horse to a stop in front of the sheriff's office. Within a few minutes, he and Becca were inside, introductions had been made, and Slade was shaking hands with Brady Webster, a handsome, well-built blond man who appeared to be about thirty.

Becca vaguely listened as Slade told Brady about everything that had happened on the Bonnie Blue, as well as his conversation with Folger. She was more intent on reliving the tremendous sense of pride she'd felt as she'd ridden through Jubele with Slade, then walked by his side into Brady's office. She'd waved breezily to several of her women friends, seeing the head-to-toe scrutiny they gave Slade. *Her* Slade.

"Fair enough," Brady said. Becca snapped her attention back to the business at hand. "Let's go over to the telegraph office. I'll tell Mrs. Whipple to have a piece of pie at the cafe. I'm glad you're here, Slade. I'm out of ideas of ways to stop Folger. He's smart, and he's mean."

"He's also a drunk," Slade said.

"That's true, but that could work for or against you. I'm not sure he's thinking clearly half the time." He turned to Becca. "So, Miss Colten, are you off to the general store while Slade and I tend to these telegrams?"

"No," Slade said. "Becca stays with me. I'll take her to the store later if she wants to go."

Brady looked at Slade, at Becca, then back at Slade. A slow smile crept onto the sheriff's face.

"I see," he said. "Well, that's clear enough."

"Good," Slade said. "Let's go."

Mrs. Whipple agreed to go for a snack of pie only after being introduced "to your handsome young man, Becca Colten." Slade tipped his hat to the elderly lady, who bustled out the door beaming and obviously eager to spread the news of Becca's beau.

"Brady," Slade said, "I need to send a telegram to the county office in Houston to check on whether or not Folger registered the Four Aces brand. Tell them we're waiting for an immediate reply."

"All right."

Slade stared out the window as they waited for the answer from Houston. Eventually the telegraph machine began to click. When it stilled, Slade smiled and nodded.

"What did they say?" Becca asked. "You two understand that clatter, but I don't."

"Folger didn't register his brand," Slade said. "We've got him now."

"But how—" she started.

"Brady," Slade went on, "send this telegram, will you? It's to Mattie Muldoon, Silver Spur Saloon, Dodge City, Kansas. Have it read, 'Don't worry. Should be over soon. Slade.'"

Brady frowned, looked quickly at Becca, then turned to the counter to do as instructed.

A strange roaring noise in Becca's ears blocked the sound of the clicking telegraph machine.

Mattie Muldoon. The words echoed in her mind with increasing force. *Mattie Muldoon.* There was a woman waiting for Slade in Dodge City, a woman who was so important to him, he'd sent her a telegram that implicitly promised he'd leave Texas and be back with her soon.

Oh, dear Lord, she thought, the man she loved, the man she'd shared exquisitely beautiful lovemaking with, the man she'd hoped and prayed would remain with her on the Bonnie Blue for all time, belonged to another woman. *Mattie Muldoon.*

"There you go, Slade," Brady said.

"All right. I'll send the last one." Slade stepped forward and operated the machine himself.

"Code?" Brady asked when Slade was done.

"Yes. Safer. That does it for now. I'll be expecting you out at the Bonnie Blue to pick up Gil."

"Fine. Miss Colten, are you feeling poorly? You're very pale all of a sudden."

"Oh, no, no, I'm fine," she said, forcing a smile. "It's just a bit stuffy in here." She wanted to go home, now. Run, now. Not face the truth about Slade and Mattie Muldoon. Her world was crumbling around her, and among the debris would be the pieces of her shattered heart. "I just need some fresh air."

"Let's get outside," Slade said. He shook hands with Brady. "Thanks for your help."

"Sure," Brady said, then glanced once more at Becca. "I'll be checking in with you, Slade."

"Yep. Come on, Becca."

She forced another weak smile and hurried out of the telegraph office.

. . .

It seemed like an eternity to Becca before she reached the sanctuary of her bedroom. Sinking onto the bed, she pressed her hands over her eyes, holding back hot tears.

Oh, God, she was such a fool, she thought. A childish, naive fool. She'd fallen in love with the wrong man. Even though Slade had told her he walked through his two worlds alone, he did, in actuality, belong to Mattie Muldoon. Why hadn't he told her before?

She narrowed her eyes in concentration. In Jubele he had made no attempt to conceal his contacting another woman. Did that mean he knew she'd placed more importance on their lovemaking than he? He'd purposely had her witness his connection to another woman because he was too cowardly to tell her straight out that he didn't, would never, love her exclusively?

She pounded the bed as her fury rose. Yes, that was the act of a coward. She may have fallen in love with the wrong man, but she would face the consequences bravely and with dignity. Her heart was crushed into a million pieces, her pride was in shambles, but Slade Ironbow would never know.

Becca lifted her chin and nodded decisively, paying no attention to the errant tear that slid slowly down her cheek.

"Holy—" Frank started as he attempted to sit up. He groaned, clutched his leg with both hands, and sank back against the pillows. "Blasted damn leg." He drew a shuddering breath, then wiped sweat from his brow. "You sure do know how to startle a man, Slade. Hell's fire, with this plan of yours, you're tempting the devil himself to come after you." He grinned. "What I wouldn't give to be going with you."

Slade shook his head. "You never did know how to stay

away from trouble, Frankie. That leg of yours is going to keep you out of this one, though."

"I know, dammit. What you're proposing is really legal?"

"Yep."

"Oh, it's a beauty of a setup."

"Yep."

"And you could get yourself killed, Slade."

"My getting killed isn't part of the plan. Never is. Frank, no one knows about this except you. I'll give Brady Webster the details when he comes out tonight to pick up Gil. No one else on the Bonnie Blue is to be told."

"What about Becca? You said you sent the telegram in code. Didn't you explain things to her during the ride back from Jubele?"

"No. I was working out the details in my mind. I didn't say anything to Becca, and she didn't ask."

"That's strange. Becca usually wants to know everything about everything."

Slade shrugged. "She was quiet, just enjoyed the ride, I guess. I don't want her to know, Frank. She'll only worry. When it's all over is soon enough to tell her."

Frank grinned again. "Don't want to upset her, huh? That's real protective of you, I must say. Yes, sir, you're sure doing a fine job taking care of Becca."

Slade frowned at Frank. "So?"

"So, I'm just stating a fact." He paused. "You figure it will be a couple of days—nights, actually—before you have everything set to go?"

"Yes. I'm telling you all this so that if anything happens to me, someone on the Bonnie Blue will have details to back up what Brady Webster says."

"The boys on the Bonnie Blue will want to be there, Slade."

"No."

"Listen to me. We all have a score to settle for what Folger did to Jed. And for busting my leg, too. The Bonnie Blue is home to us, and Jed Colten was one of the finest men I've ever known. These boys deserve the right to be there when Folger pays."

Slade ran his hand over the back of his neck. "Folger has hired guns, Frank. The Bonnie Blue men can shoot, but they're cowboys first. Gunfighters usually don't know a heifer from a horse, but they can put a bullet in a man's heart before a cowboy can clear leather."

"Dammit, Slade, don't leave them out of this. Jed Colten was our friend. Every man here is proud to be a part of the Bonnie Blue. You'd be stripping them of their pride if the score with Folger was settled without them taking part in it. They've earned the right to be there."

His eyes narrowed, Slade looked at Frank for a long moment. "All right," he said finally. "I'll tell them just before I'm ready to go, and each man can make his own decision. I won't think less of anyone who chooses to stay behind."

"Every one of them will saddle up, Slade, you'll see. Lord knows I'd be right there with you if I could." Frank frowned. "There's something else you ought to think on. Jed was Becca's father. She loved her pa, and she loves the ranch. I'm not saying she should ride with you when you do this, but she deserves to know what you're doing. She's a Colten, and this is Colten land. Tell her."

Slade stood up. "No."

"You sure don't understand women much," Frank said, shaking his head.

"Never claimed to," Slade muttered as he left.

Oh, Lord, Frank thought. Becca's going to give him hell when this is over.

As he walked out of the bunkhouse, the beauty of the Bonnie Blue struck Slade anew. Another magnificent sunset had painted the sky, and everywhere he looked, lush, fertile land stretched to the horizon. This land called his name as the wind once had, and it did not force him to choose between his two worlds. He had found his place—the place where he could work hard and enjoy the fruits of his labors. Where he could sink his hands into the rich soil, feel it and savor it, instead of trying to catch the elusive whisper of the wind.

Yes, Slade thought, he was home.

He turned, sweeping his gaze over the majestic house. Becca was in there, bringing to the rooms the sound of her laughter, the raging of her temper, the sunshine of her spirit. He loved her laughter, her fiery temper. He loved her.

Slade stiffened, every muscle in his body tensed nearly to the point of pain. In his mind he could hear her name chanted by Indian braves to the rhythm of ceremonial drums. She would stand by his side as his father, following traditions as old as time, joined them, declared them husband and wife.

And he heard her name sung by a choir as she walked down the aisle of a church, wearing a delicate white dress and veil. She'd place her hand in his, and they'd repeat the sacred vows, pledging their love until death parted them. He'd slip a gold band onto her finger and wear a matching one on his own.

Two ceremonies uniting them. Two worlds to which they belonged, as would the children they created.

Slade stared up at the heavens for a long moment to gain control of his thoughts and emotions. Tonight, he decided, he would talk to Becca, say all the words that echoed in his mind and heart. She cared deeply for him, he was sure of it. He'd nurture that caring into a love that would match his.

He was pulled from his reverie by the sound of approaching horses. The men of the Bonnie Blue were riding in, a billow of dust accompanying them. He stared at the house for another long moment, then strode toward the barn. Business first.

After talking with Yancey about the work done on the ranch that day, Slade headed for the house. At the pump he stripped off his hat and shirt, then splashed cold water over his head and chest. He dried with the thin flour-sack towel that hung over the pump, then reached for his shirt.

He paused, though, remembering that Becca hadn't come out of the house since they'd returned from town. That meant she was probably still wearing her pretty yellow dress. He'd do well to put on a clean shirt, spruce up a bit.

After all, he reasoned, it was a special occasion when a man declared his love for a woman and asked her to be his wife. It definitely called for a clean shirt.

A short time later, he entered the dining room wearing a royal-blue western shirt, his damp hair neatly combed. Becca's door had been closed when he'd passed it on his way downstairs, but he'd hoped she'd be waiting for him in the dining room, a smile on her face. Instead, he found Maria placing a platter of pork chops in the center of the table.

"Hello, Maria. Where's Becca?"

"I'll go check her room. I've been busy in the pantry and haven't seen her. She may have napped after you came back from Jubele. I'll just go make sure she's awake and ready to eat."

"That won't be necessary," Becca said.

Slade and Maria looked over to the doorway. Slade's eyes widened for an instant, then narrowed as he frowned.

Becca was clad in worn, faded blue jeans and an equally faded tan shirt. She'd braided her hair into a single plait, then twisted it into a tight figure eight at the back of her head. Her face was pale, and there was no hint of a smile on her lips.

"For mercy sake," Maria said, "you look like last week's ragbag. Why did you change out of your nice dress?"

"These clothes are comfortable," Becca said, sitting down at the head of the table. "Besides, it isn't as though this is a special meal. There's only me"—she slid a cool glance at Slade—"and my foreman."

Fourteen

The sudden cold in the dining room made it feel as if a winter storm had swept through. What was only seconds, seemed to Becca like torturously long minutes before Maria gasped, breaking the icy silence.

"Becca," she scolded, "what a way to talk. What's wrong with you?"

"Wrong?" Becca repeated. "Nothing is wrong. Slade *is* the foreman of the Bonnie Blue. The temporary foreman, of course. Isn't that right, Mr. Ironbow?"

Becca looked at Maria, resisting the temptation to turn to Slade. She jumped slightly when, out of the corner of her eye, she caught the motion of his chair being pulled out. Slade sat down.

"Becca," Maria said sternly, "I don't know what bee you've gotten in your bonnet, but there's no call for—"

"Maria," Slade interrupted. His voice was expressionless. "The food looks delicious. Thank you."

Maria looked at him for a long moment, then stomped

out of the room, muttering under her breath. Slade began to fill his plate. Becca stared at her empty one.

"Potatoes?" he asked, holding out the bowl to her.

"Yes, thank you." She kept her eyes averted from his as she reached for the bowl.

He moved the bowl away and grasped her hand with his free one. She stiffened in surprise.

"I've been told," he said, "that I don't understand women, and I've never claimed that I do. So, you're going to have to spell it out for me, Becca."

"To what are you referring?" she asked, staring at his large hand engulfing hers.

"Look at me."

"Slade—"

"Dammit, Becca, look at me!"

Her head snapped up, her eyes narrowed with anger. "Don't tell me what to do, Slade Ironbow. What's next? You send me to my room like a naughty little girl? I am not a child! I'm a woman, who knows her own mind."

"Believe me, I'm very aware that you're a woman," he said. "Now, suppose you tell me what's going on in that woman's mind of yours."

She tried to tug her hand free, but he refused to release it. "May I have my hand back?" she asked stiffly.

"No. I want an answer from you. Something obviously happened today to get you mad as a hornet, but I sure as hell don't know what it is."

"And I sure as hell am not going to tell you. You know as well as I exactly what it is. I understand facts when they're presented to me, sir."

"What facts?" he shouted.

She yanked her hand free and plopped a mound of mashed potatoes on her plate. She added a pork chop and a generous serving of carrots. The knot in her stomach tightened, but she forced herself to take a bite of the potatoes and swallow them past the lump in her throat.

Do not cry, she told herself firmly. Dignity, Becca. Remember your pride.

Slade leaned back in his chair and stared at Becca. What in the hell was the matter with her? he wondered. He'd been planning on asking her to marry him, and now it appeared he'd do better to ask her not to shoot him.

He shook his head and turned his attention to his food. They ate in stony silence, neither really tasting their dinner. Slade finally pushed his empty plate away and folded his arms on the table.

"Ready to talk about it now?" he asked.

She put down her fork and reached for her coffee cup. "There's nothing to talk about." She took a sip of coffee, then replaced the cup in the china saucer. "I presumed too much, that's all," she went on, her voice trembling slightly. "A mistake, but one I've corrected. You have nothing to worry about, Slade. I have no intention of creating a scene."

"What," he asked, sweeping one arm through the air, "would you call this? You're talking, but not saying a damn thing. I can't read your mind, Becca. Something has upset you, but I can't fix it because I don't have the slightest clue as to what it is. Stop acting like a pouting child and tell me what's going on here."

"Pouting—Oh, you despicable man." She jumped to her feet. "I'd like a full report from you in the morning as to your plans for dealing with Folger. Plans that I know you have, and as soon as you execute them you can return to—" She stopped speaking and started toward the door.

Slade lunged to his feet. "Return to where?" he yelled.

She halted and glanced back at him. "Isn't the 'whom' more important? Why are you acting so surprised? You intended for me to get that terribly subtle message that you're involved with her."

"Her? Her who?"

"Damn you," she cried. "Mattie Muldoon!" With that she ran from the room.

"Mattie . . . Oh, holy hell," Slade said under his breath. "The telegram."

"Oh, mercy," Maria whispered, coming into the room.

Slade sat down heavily in his chair.

"Slade," Maria asked, "where did Becca hear Mattie's name?"

"I sent Mattie a telegram saying not to worry, that things would be over here soon. I never thought about how Becca might interpret it. Oh, hell, Maria, I can't explain it to her, tell Becca who Mattie really is. If I say that Mattie is just a friend, the person I'm paying the debt to Jed Colten for, Becca will press for details."

"That she will," Maria said, fiddling with her apron. "But as it stands, Becca thinks that you and Mattie are . . . Mercy me, Slade, what are you going to do?"

"Damned if I know," he said, pushing himself to his feet. "My life was a helluva lot less complicated before I met Becca Colten. Women! They'll put a man in an early grave."

Shaking her head, Maria watched Slade leave, his heavy strides rattling the china on the table.

To Becca, the night seemed endless. Nightmares plagued her sleep, waking her often. As she dressed in pants and a work shirt the next morning, weariness swept over her. Her eyes felt gritty with fatigue. How easy it would be, she mused, to plead illness and not ride with Slade that day. But she had no intention of cowering under the blankets. She knew about Mattie Muldoon, Slade knew she knew, and that was that.

"Good morning, Maria," she said, forcing a cheerful smile as she entered the kitchen. She glanced at the table and frowned when she saw that Slade wasn't in his usual chair. "Not much breakfast for me, please. I'm not very hungry."

Maria turned from the stove to look at Becca. "All I'm going to say to you is that things aren't always as they seem."

"Oh? And then again," Becca said, an edge to her voice, "more often than not, things are exactly as they appear to be. We do better to face the facts as they are."

"As you may *think* they are," Maria said, waggling a wooden spoon at her. "No, I won't say another word. It's not my place to explain about—No, no, not another word."

"You're not making a great deal of sense this morning. I think the subject is best dropped. I made a mistake in judgment. I'm not the first woman, nor will I be the last, to do that."

Maria sighed. "Oh, honey, you don't understand that—" A knock sounded at the back door. "Now, who's that at breakfast time?" She crossed the room and opened the door. " 'Morning, Bucky. What brings you up to the house so early?"

"Got a message from Mr. Ironbow for Miss Colten," Bucky said, then snatched his hat from his head. "Mr. Ironbow said Miss Colten was to ride with Pete and Cody today, and stay with 'em while they do whatever they're doin' out on the range. Mr. Ironbow said he's got some business to tend to."

"What kind of business, Bucky?" Becca asked.

"Can't rightly say, ma'am, 'cause he didn't tell me. Just said I should deliver the message to you like I did."

"I see. Slade rode out alone?"

"Yes, ma'am."

She took a deep breath in an attempt to control her anger.

"After giving strict instructions that everyone stay in pairs, he rode out alone?"

Bucky twisted his hat in his hands. "Well . . . um, yes,

ma'am, but then he's the foreman, you know, so there's nobody goin' to give him fits about breakin' his own rule or nothing. He did say, too, that he wasn't sure when he'd be back so not to wait supper for him this evening if he wasn't here in time to sit down to the table. Well, I best go have my breakfast so I'll be ready to ride out with the boys."

"Yes, of course. Thank you, Bucky. I'll be along shortly." She closed the door and spun around to face Maria. "Did you hear that, Maria? Slade is out there alone. Why? He's getting ready to make some kind of move against Henry Folger, isn't he?"

"I don't know," Maria said. "Sit down there now, and have some breakfast. The boys will be fixing to ride out soon, and I'm assuming you'll want to be with them."

"Yes, of course I will," Becca said absently. Where had Slade gone, and to do what? Was it simply an excuse to keep out of her way in the hope that time would cool her raging temper about Mattie Muldoon? Somehow she didn't think so. Slade was working out the details of a plan to stop Folger, and he was out there alone. He had to be careful and come home safely.

She forced a smile as Maria placed a plate in front of her; then she ate her eggs without tasting them. Slade wasn't going to come home, she thought dismally. Not really. That had been a pipe dream that had gone up like a puff of smoke from a dying fire. Reality was in Dodge City, Kansas. Reality's name was Mattie Muldoon.

Mattie bent over the button bin in the rear of Widow Sullivan's store and poked through the dozens of buttons. She'd promised Abe she'd replace the one he'd lost on his favorite shirt.

The Widow Sullivan had nodded stiffly to Mattie when she entered the store, and then had totally ignored her.

Mattie was accustomed to such behavior, and didn't give it a moment's thought. As she delved deeper into the button bin, she was vaguely aware of the brass bell tinkling over the door, announcing the arrival of more customers. She ignored the sound of women's voices, until she heard her name.

"It's a disgrace," the woman was saying, "that Doc Willis is courting her. Why, I was just making plans to have the good doctor to Sunday supper to sit across the table proper from my Luellen. My daughter has blossomed into such a beauty, and she's come of age, you know, Sara Beth."

"Well," Sara Beth said, "your Luellen is a very . . . unique-appearing young woman, Maralynn. However, I'm convinced Doc is determined to win the heart of Mattie Muldoon." She sighed. "I've daydreamed about having hair the color of Mattie Muldoon's. Oh, she does have beautiful hair."

"Sara Beth, for shame. How can you praise such a wanton woman? I'm surprised at you. Shocked, as well."

"I find no fault in admiring Mattie Muldoon's hair, Maralynn," Sara Beth said indignantly. "The truth be known, I think she has a fine figure, too, just as trim and pretty as you please. Me? Six babes born and I look like a loaf of sourdough bread. Can't say I blame Doc Willis for pursuing her."

Maralynn gasped with horror. "Sara Beth, she is a fallen woman."

"Oh, pshaw. Just whose kettle are you calling black, Maralynn? I happen to know that that fancy fringed lamp you just bought was paid for by money your Elmer won playing poker at the Silver Spur."

"There is no call to mention that," Maralynn said, tilting her nose in the air.

Mattie straightened and walked toward the front of the store. Both women stared at her with chagrin. "No call to mention," Mattie asked, "that your Elmer drops by the Spur nearly every night? I can't help but wonder why that is acceptable, but my owning the Spur is not."

"Good question," Sara Beth said.

"Sara Beth!" Maralynn exclaimed, pressing her hand over her heart. "I will pray for your soul as I'm praying for Doc Willis's. I must get home and lie down. I feel faint, I truly do." She hurried out of the store.

Sara Beth looked at Mattie. "Mattie Muldoon, if you pass up the chance to find happiness with a fine man like Doc Willis, then you're not the woman of strength I believe you to be. I trust you're even capable of convincing Slade Ironbow not to shoot Doc dead, too. And I still say you have the most beautiful hair I've ever seen."

Mattie smiled at her. "Thank you, Sara Beth."

"So? Are you going to let the narrow-minded gossips of Dodge dictate your future happiness?"

Mattie lifted her chin and squared her shoulders. "I certainly am not. I love Jim Willis. If this town won't accept us as husband and wife, then we'll just go somewhere else."

"Good for you," Sara Beth said. "You best go tell Doc Willis the joyous news. That poor man has moved heaven and earth to win your heart." She paused. "Mattie, I wish you every happiness. I've lived in Dodge many years, and it hurts me to see so many people standing in judgment of you. Oh, the stories I could tell about many of those folks and their wild, young days. There's not one among us who doesn't have something best left buried in the past. What's important is today and the tomorrows."

"You're right," Mattie said. "Thank you, Sara Beth."

Widow Sullivan lumbered over to them. "Thank you? What did I miss here, Sara Beth? I didn't know you were on chatting terms with Mattie Muldoon."

"I most certainly am," Sara Beth said. "Mattie, go tend

to that business we discussed. Widow Sullivan, there's going to be a wedding in Dodge City."

One hour later, Mattie made no attempt to hide her smile as she rode straight down the center of the main street of Dodge. She was driving the same fancy buggy that Doc had used to take her on their picnic. A buzz of voices followed her, and she kept the horse at a slow, plodding pace, determined that no one would miss seeing her.

She held her head high, and her smile was genuine. She felt young and carefree, ready to set aside and forget the trials and heartaches of the past. She would lift her face to the warm sunshine of the tomorrows spent with the man she loved.

Near the end of the street, she halted the horse in front of Doc's office. He must have been aware of some commotion, for he stepped outside almost immediately. A hush fell over the throng of people. No one wanted to miss one word of what Doc and Mattie would say.

"Miss Muldoon," Doc said, a wide smile on his face, "this is indeed a pleasant surprise. I take it you've come to call?"

"I've come, Jim Willis," Mattie said, her voice clear and strong, "to accept your proposal of marriage."

A gasp went up from the uninvited audience.

"Mattie?" he said, searching her face intently.

"It's true, Jim. If you still want me, I'd be honored to be your wife. And, if you feel so inclined, I have a picnic lunch here so that we can celebrate our betrothal. Sir?"

"Mattie Muldoon," Doc yelled, spreading his arms wide, "I love you! Dodge City, say hello to the future Mrs. James Willis!" He bounded up onto the buggy seat, gave Mattie a fast, hard kiss, then took the reins from her hands.

Many of the spectators cheered, while others clucked with disapproval.

"What about Slade Ironbow, Doc?" someone called.

Doc laughed. "We'll ask him to stand up for us as our witness." He flicked the reins, urging the horse to a trot. "Oh, Mattie," he said quietly as Dodge fell behind, "this is the happiest day of my life."

"I love you, Jim," she said, smiling at him with sparkling eyes. "It's time to look forward to our future, not wallow in the misery of the past. We'll start fresh, wherever you choose, but I do think we should leave Dodge."

"Then leave we will. When will you marry me, Mattie? Yesterday? Today?"

"The minute Slade gets back," she said, laughing. "He's our dear friend, and I'd really like him to be at our wedding." She paused, her smile fading. "Jim, forgive me for not being as strong as I thought I was. Fear nearly kept me from reaching out to you, telling you how I truly felt about you. I do love you so very much."

"And that's all we need . . . our love."

She rested her head on his shoulder as they rode to their private, secluded place filled with wildflowers.

Fifteen

There was no sign of Slade at supper that evening. Becca sat alone at the big table and poked at her food, her gaze continually drawn to Slade's empty chair.

Where was he? What business had he needed to tend to? What was taking so long, keeping him out there alone instead of returning to the Bonnie Blue?

She sighed and told herself to get used to looking at that empty chair. Soon Slade would leave for good, returning to his precious Mattie Muldoon.

Oh, why hadn't he told her about Mattie before she'd fallen in love with him? Why hadn't he told her before he'd made love to her? She frowned, nudging a piece of meat around on her plate. For that matter, why had he made love to her at all if he was in love with another woman? She knew men sometimes took their pleasure where they found it, but now that her temper had cooled, she had to admit Slade would never use her like that.

171

So . . . could it be that whatever his connection to this Mattie Muldoon, he didn't actually love her? Could she simply be a special friend, someone—

"Oh, no," Becca whispered, sitting up straight. Someone Slade would repay a debt for? Could Mattie Muldoon be the friend indebted to Jed Colten?

"But why didn't he tell me?" she wailed.

Because you didn't give him the chance, she answered herself. She'd leaped to a conclusion, condemning him without giving him the chance to explain.

Now what did she do? It was rather difficult to ask a man a question when he wasn't there to answer it. How dare Slade just up and go off alone with no regard for her peace of mind? Where was he? What was he doing? Oh, the questions. The seemingly never-ending questions.

With a sigh, Becca left the dining room. As she wearily climbed the stairs to her bedroom, she decided the house was too big, too empty, and too lonely without Slade.

After supper the next day, Becca restlessly paced the length of the large living room. There had been no word from Slade, nothing, and her stomach was twisted into an increasingly painful knot.

Although she was worried sick about Slade, not one other person on the Bonnie Blue felt there was any cause for concern. Everyone agreed that Slade could take care of himself and that he'd return to the Bonnie Blue when he'd finished whatever it was he had to do.

Their confidence in Slade, perversely, heightened her anxiety.

"Dammit," she whispered, "where is he?"

"Becca."

She spun around at the sound of her name being spoken in that rich, deep voice.

Slade stood in the doorway to the living room. He was home.

She swept her gaze over him, drinking in every rugged, dusty inch of him. He looked tired, he was obviously dirty from many hours spent wherever it was that he'd been, and he certainly wasn't greeting her with a warm smile.

He was absolutely beautiful.

"You're back," she said. Oh, Becca, she chided herself, what a stupid thing to say. Still, it was better than flinging herself into his arms so she could be assured he was really there.

He nodded sharply. "I'm meeting with the men outside the barn in half an hour. I need to clean up a bit, then get something to eat. If you want to hear what I have to say, be there."

She started to reply, only to blink in surprise as he strode away without another word.

"Well!" she exclaimed. Well . . . fine. She'd most certainly be outside to hear just what Slade Ironbow had to say for himself. He should be reporting to her first, since what he had to say obviously involved the ranch, but she wouldn't quibble about that.

A soft smile curved her lips as she stared at the doorway where he had stood. There was every chance, she knew, that it was over between her and Slade, that he would ride away from the Bonnie Blue, back to the welcoming, loving embrace of Mattie Muldoon. There was every chance that Becca was destined to cry lonely tears as she attempted to repair her shattered heart.

But at that moment, that glorious moment, Slade was home.

Slade finished speaking and a hush fell over the group gathered outside the barn.

"But . . ." Becca started, breaking the almost eerie silence. She pressed one hand on her jumpy stomach and took a steadying breath. "It's a dangerous plan, but it's brilliant. We can do it. We can beat Folger."

Slade glanced at her and nodded, then redirected his attention to the men. "There's one more thing I want to say to you. Not one among you will be thought less of if you don't come along tonight. You're cowhands hired on to work this land. You're not fast guns like the crew at Four Aces, and no one is expecting you to be. Come or stay, you're Bonnie Blue men, and you'll always have a place here.

"If you're going," he went on, glancing at the darkening sky, "be saddled up and ready to ride in fifteen minutes. If you're staying here, pick a spot in the shadows of the trees near the ranch house. A little extra protection for Becca and Maria won't hurt."

"What?" Becca said.

"We're staying here, Becca," Maria said.

"No, I'm—"

"Hush," Maria said sharply. "You listen to me, Becca Colten. I watched your pa start the Bonnie Blue with nothing more than a strong back and a dream. When Bonnie died, he kept on working this land from dawn to dusk to leave a legacy for you. All those years, all that backbreaking labor, and the Bonnie Blue is one of the finest ranches in Texas. You owe it to your pa to keep yourself safe this night. Henry Folger is going to pay for killing Jed Colten, and when it's finished, there will still be a Colten standing on Bonnie Blue land. Don't fight Slade on this, honey. You and I will go up to the house and wait for the Bonnie Blue men to come home."

Again a silence fell over the group, broken only by the sounds of small night creatures emerging under the cloak of darkness.

Becca looked at each of the men, meeting their gazes, receiving their nods and smiles. Slade's eyes were shadowed by his Stetson, and she had no clue as to what he was thinking.

Seconds ticked slowly by.

She lifted her chin, gazing directly at Slade. "Yes," she said softly, "we'll wait at the house. We'll wait for the Bonnie Blue men to come home."

Murmurs of approval buzzed among the men, then Slade raised one hand for silence.

"How many of you are staying here?"

"Not this man," a voice called. "Move, you lazy cowboys, I've got a meetin' with a rattlesnake."

All gazes were on the barn door as a small wagon emerged with Bucky sitting on the wooden seat, holding the reins. In the back of the wagon, his splinted leg propped on top of a mound of pillows, was a grinning Frank Tatum.

Slade chuckled. "Like I've said, Frankie, you never could stay out of trouble. You're going to Folger's?"

"Damn straight I am," Frank said. "I owe him double. Jed Colten was my friend, and I happen to be mighty fond of this leg of mine. Yeah, Slade, I'm going to Folger's."

"Fair enough," Slade said. "So? Who's staying here?"

No one spoke.

Slade pushed his Stetson to the back of his head and frowned. "I hope I made it clear that there's no shame in not going to Four Aces. Yancey?"

"You can order me to stay put, Slade, if you think I'm too old to pull my weight, but I'm not volunteerin' to stay behind. From what I can see here, all these boys are going to be saddled up and ready to ride."

Slade paused, studying the men, and then he nodded. "All right. Saddle up."

A current of anticipation crackled through the air as the men ran into the barn. The time had come; the waiting was over. Folger was going to pay for killing Jed

Colten and for breaking Frank's leg. This night belonged to the men of the Bonnie Blue.

"I'll see you into the house," Slade said, jerking his head at Becca and Maria. "My horse is saddled and ready to go. Come on."

"That's very gentlemanly of you, Slade," Maria said, starting toward the house. "Don't you think so, Becca?"

Becca hesitated for just a moment, allowing Slade to join her, then fell in step alongside him. Neither spoke, but for just a moment their eyes met. Slade faltered, overwhelmed by the need to pull her into his arms and tell her he loved her. But that would have to wait for later, when he could explain everything.

He quickened his pace. "Promise me you'll stay inside."

"Promise me you'll be careful at Folger's, Slade. What you're about to do is dangerous. Folger is going to be furious. He'll go crazy with anger."

"Don't worry, Becca, I have all the details worked out. You have to remember that we have the element of surprise on our side, too. Folger isn't expecting what is about to happen."

"I realize that, but . . ."

They reached the kitchen door. He opened it and stepped back for her to enter. He followed her inside, but didn't close the door. Maria was nowhere in sight.

"We'll be back as soon as we can, Becca."

"I'll be waiting—" She stopped. She mustn't say it, she told herself. Even though the words "I'll be waiting for you" were aching to burst from her lips, she dared not say them. Not yet. "Please, be careful, Slade."

"I will." He lifted one hand as if to touch her face, then dropped it back to his side. "We'll talk, Becca, when this thing with Folger is over."

He turned and left, closing the door behind him.

Becca stood in the quiet room and pressed her fingertips to her lips, willing herself not to cry.

"Come in and sit in the living room," Maria said quietly from the kitchen doorway. "All we can do now is wait."

Becca stared at the door that Slade had gone through, then nodded. She turned and followed Maria from the kitchen, not attempting to speak past the ache of tears in her throat.

The moon inched its way higher in the sky, guiding the riders from the Bonnie Blue over the dark land. Not far from Four Aces, a single rider emerged from the shadows of a group of mesquite trees and pulled his horse in next to Slade's.

"Brady," Slade said, nodding.

"Slade. Looks like all the Bonnie Blue is here."

"Yep."

"Figured they would be. Miss Colten and Maria?"

"At the house."

Brady chuckled. "You must have done some quick talkin' to convince Miss Colten to stay behind. I expected her to be right up front with you here."

"No. I didn't like leaving her and Maria alone in the house, but these men have the right to go to Four Aces."

"That's a fact, Slade. Miss Colten and Maria will be fine at the ranch. We're going to be keeping Folger and his boys too busy to be wondering where Becca Colten is."

Slade raised one hand to halt the slowly moving group. "Cody," he said, "throw a rope over that notched post there, and pull it free so we can get through. I've got it resting easy, so it won't take much to clear the barbed wire in that section."

"You've been busy, Slade," Yancey said as Cody did as instructed.

"We're about to get busier. We're going in the back way, like I said, over that rise. The house and bunkhouse aren't far from the base of it, and there's a stand of trees and a small hill we can use for protection if they start shooting. At the bottom of the rise, spread out in a line. Have your rifle ready, but no one, *no one*, fires unless I give the word. Questions?" He paused. "Let's go."

Slade urged his horse to a canter, and the other men kept time with him. A thin cloud streaked in front of the moon, partially blocking the silvery luminescence and casting shifting shadows over the men and horses.

No one spoke. They crossed the Four Aces land and took up their positions with a precision that could have been born of hours of rehearsal, but came instead from pure determination to succeed in their mission.

Slade turned in his saddle to see the line of Bonnie Blue men stretched out behind him, each cowhand sitting straight and tall, his rifle across his thighs. The well-trained quarter horses were all motionless.

"Ready?" Slade asked Brady.

"Anytime you are," the sheriff said.

The pair nudged their horses to about fifteen feet in front of the others, then stopped. Brady pulled out his rifle, but Slade left his in the boot of his saddle.

"Four Aces," he called to the lighted bunkhouse, "this is Ironbow from the Bonnie Blue. We want to speak to Folger."

Voices raised in surprise could immediately be heard from the bunkhouse, and moments later men barreled out the door, rifles in hands.

"There's no need for gunfire," Slade said. "All we want is a few words with Folger."

"He don't want to talk to you, Ironbow," Casey yelled. "You take your cow-dungers and get off this ranch."

" 'Evenin', Casey," Slade said calmly. "This is Sheriff Webster. Have you met the sheriff? He's here to see that this is carried out nice and legal."

"What in the hell are you talkin' about?" Casey asked.

"You're trespassing, Ironbow. Folger is mighty particular 'bout who comes on Four Aces land."

"We won't be here long," Slade said. "We're just going to round up the cattle—What do you have? Two, three thousand head?—and move 'em on over to the Bonnie Blue."

"What!" Casey roared. The men behind him shouted angry curses. "You're crazy. Get out of here before you got nothin' to take with you except dead cowboys slung over their saddles. You can't steal Four Aces cattle. You're facing some of the best guns in Texas."

"I wasn't planning on stealing anything, Casey. The cattle on this land are public domain. They're ours, or anyone else's, for the taking because Folger didn't register his brand. The Four Aces brand is worthless. Without the stock, this ranch is just about worthless too. We're taking the cattle . . . now. You might go deliver that message to Folger. He's finished here. He's about to lose every head of beef he thought he owned. Four Aces is no longer a working ranch."

"The hell you say!" a voice boomed.

Slade narrowed his eyes as he watched Henry Folger lumber across the expanse of grass behind the house. He stopped beside Casey, and Slade could see the sweat dripping from Folger's florid face.

"Get off my land!" Folger bellowed.

"We intend to," Slade said, "but we're taking the cattle with us. You should have registered that brand, Folger."

"It's all legal," Brady Webster added. "You didn't follow the law, Henry. Cattle without a registered brand are public domain and can belong to any man who chooses to claim them. You're losing your beef stock. The way I see it, you'll lose Four Aces next. Can't say as anyone will miss you around here."

"Shut up, Webster," Folger snapped. "Ironbow, you've got three seconds to order those Bonnie Blue men off my land, or I'll give the word to open fire. You don't stand a chance against my guns."

"Don't do it, Folger," Slade said. "You can't win."

Folger laughed, the harsh sound more like a sneer. "Oh, I'll win, and I'll have the sweet Becca as part of the prize. You'll be dead, alongside the sheriff and every one of those cowboys of yours. Nice bluff, Ironbow, but it didn't work. Trained guns have the final word."

Slade took off his Stetson, circled it once over his head, then tugged it back into place.

"No," he said. "Fast guns aren't always the answer, Folger."

"Holy hell, what's that?" Casey suddenly exclaimed. "Look! Up on the rise, those lights . . . They're torches. Holy hell, Folger, there's a whole row of Indians coming over that rise. Indians, for God's sake!"

Brady turned to look at the Indians moving into place behind the Bonnie Blue men. Each one held a burning torch, and it cast an eerie orange glow over the entire area.

"Impressive," Brady said quietly to Slade.

Slade chuckled. "My father loves a good show. Brings back memories for him."

"I'm getting out of here, Folger," Casey said, backing away. The men behind him started doing the same. "I'm not takin' on no Indians."

"Open fire, you fool," Folger commanded. "Kill them, all of them. I don't want one man from the Bonnie Blue or one Indian left alive. And shoot Webster, too."

"That's not very neighborly," Brady muttered.

"Damn you, shoot them!" Folger shrieked.

"No," Casey said. "I'm getting the hell out of here right now."

Folger yanked the rifle from Casey's hand and opened fire on the double line of men before him. The action jolted some of the Four Aces men, and they began to fire too. The Bonnie Blue men and the Indians spread out, firing as they headed for the shadows.

Even as the Indians quickly extinguished their torches, riderless horses scattered in all directions. Bucky hustled the horse pulling the wagon, calling to the animal to hurry out of the way, while Frank swore and clutched his splinted leg.

It was chaos. The sound of gunfire echoed around them, and reddish flashes from numerous rifles lit the night. Indians and Bonnie Blue men dove for the protection of the trees and the hill, as some of the Four Aces crew ran for the barn to get their horses and escape.

Crouched close to the ground, Slade hurried from one Bonnie Blue man to the next. He urged them not to shoot to kill, but if it became necessary, not to hesitate in order to protect themselves. He found the men calm, and very determined to be victorious.

In the shadows of the trees, he met his father.

"Enju, my son, it is good," Chief Lone Eagle said, beaming. "You bring joy to our people by including us in this battle."

"I was hoping it wouldn't come to firing," Slade said. "Folger will never give the order to cease fire."

"Perhaps we should change his mind," Lone Eagle said. "The barn we do not touch, for it holds the precious gift of animals. But the bunkhouse? The ranch house? Do you have use for these?"

"No," Slade said.

His father smiled and nodded, then disappeared into the darkness. Slade continued checking the Bonnie Blue men, and was relieved to find no one had been hurt.

The rifle fire continued, and he searched for a way to break through the line of Four Aces men to get to Folger. He didn't have to, though.

As if by magic, flaming arrows streaked through the sky in high arcs. They found their targets—the roofs of the bunkhouse and ranch house. A roar of anger and fear went up from the men of Four Aces as the buildings caught fire, lighting the sky as bright as day.

Bent over, Brady ran over to Slade. "We got 'em now. They're panicking. Those hired guns didn't sign up to take on something like this. Slade? What's wrong? You look ready to do murder."

"Dammit," Slade swore in a voice as hard as steel. "He's gone."

"What?"

"Folger. He was there, but now . . . Take over here. I've got to go. *Damn* him."

"Slade, what are you talking about?"

"The man is crazy. He won't accept defeat this easily, and even drunk he's smart. I've got to get over there."

"Over where?"

"To the Bonnie Blue. I can feel it in my gut, Brady. Folger's gone after Becca!"

Sixteen

When Becca heard the first shot fired in the distance, her eyes widened in horror. She grabbed a rifle from the rack in the entryway, then she and Maria double-checked the locks on all the doors and windows.

As the gunfire increased, Becca forced aside the frightening scenes her mind seemed determined to create.

"They'll be fine, Maria," she said. "All of the Bonnie Blue men will be fine. They're good shots, and they keep calm under pressure." She sat down next to Maria on the sofa in the living room and patted the older woman's hand. "Don't worry."

Maria nodded. "And we mustn't forget that Slade has a mighty big surprise up his sleeve for that Henry Folger. Imagine, Indians riding in to help our Bonnie Blue boys."

"Yes," Becca said softly. "Chief Lone Eagle sounds as though he's quite a man. Just like . . ." Her voice trailed off.

"His son?"

"This isn't the time to talk about Slade, Maria." She ran one fingertip over the smooth wood of the stock of the rifle. "All I can think about now is that gunfire we're hearing, and what might be happening at Four Aces." She drew a shuddering breath. "I know I said that I wanted Folger to pay for killing my pa, but . . . oh, Maria, not at the cost of innocent men's lives. My father would never have wanted that."

"Hush, Becca. Those boys had the choice to go or stay. They saddled up because they all thought highly of your pa, even those who haven't been here long."

"And Slade Ironbow?" Becca asked. "He didn't even know my father." She stood and began to pace, the rifle cradled in her arms. "Whose debt is Slade paying? Mattie Muldoon's? If that's true, then what did my father do for her that was so important?"

"Becca, you said yourself that this isn't the time to be dwelling on all that. You and Slade can talk it through when—"

She stopped when Becca abruptly held up one hand.

"Maria, did you just hear a horse gallop up to the front of the house?" Becca whispered.

"No," Maria said, getting to her feet. "That gunfire seems so loud that—Oh, my God!"

With an explosive sound, the front door shattered, splintered wood spraying in all directions. In the next instant, Henry Folger burst into the room, a revolver in one hand.

In one quick glance Becca saw the sweat and grime on Folger's clothes, the unnatural flush to his skin, and the sneering curl of his lips. His breath came in heaving gulps, and even from across the room, she could smell the rancid odor of liquor.

"Drop the rifle, Miss Becca," he said. "Unless, of course, you'd like to see your dear Maria shot dead before your eyes."

"No, no," Becca said, laying the rifle on the sofa. "How

dare you burst in here like this." She squared her shoulders and stared straight at him. "What do you want?"

"Ah, what do I want?" He laughed. Becca shivered as the strange sound hung ominously in the air. "I want that half-breed Indian to pay for what he's done to me, that's what I want, my sweet Becca. He trespassed onto my land with his useless cowboys and that stupid sheriff, and with those Indians, who are burning my house to the ground. They'll leave me nothing! Do you hear me? Nothing. What good is land when the stock is gone? Worthless. Why should a Folger have to register his brand? That's insane. Everyone knows me, everyone knows the importance of Henry Folger and Four Aces. Ironbow has made a terrible mistake, my sweet Becca, and he's going to pay dearly for it."

"I'm not your sweet Becca! Don't call me that."

"Becca, be careful," Maria whispered.

Becca took a deep breath to calm herself. "Henry, you've got to stop and think for a minute. What is happening at Four Aces is within the law, because you didn't register your brand. Even more, Slade and Brady have evidence that will prove you killed my father. You should be riding as far as you can, as fast as you can, not standing here in my living room."

"You wish me to leave, my sweet Becca?" Folger said. "Why, how very inhospitable of you. I'm the man who wanted to marry you, honor you by giving you the Folger name. You would have been mistress of Four Aces—once combined with the Bonnie Blue, the biggest, finest, most prestigious ranch in all of Texas." He shook his head and clucked his tongue. "Why did you fight me on this, sweet Becca? We could have had so much. You are a foolish child."

"And you are a murderer, Henry Folger!" Becca yelled. "You killed my father. You broke Frank Tatum's leg. Lord only knows what else you would have done if Slade hadn't come."

"Oh, yes, the great Slade Ironbow," Folger sneered. "I'll have my revenge before I leave Texas. That half-breed has taken all that I had. Well, he stood in my living room and spoke of you, and I know without a shadow of a doubt that Ironbow is in love with you, Becca Colten. And so I will take what he considers to be his." He jerked the gun at Becca. "Let's go. You're coming with me, my sweet Becca."

"I'm not going anywhere with you, Henry Folger," she said, crossing her arms over her breasts. "And you're wrong about Slade. He won't care if you take me with you. There's nothing between us. He was hired to do a job here, and that's what he's doing. He has a special woman waiting for him in Dodge City."

"You're lying," Folger said, narrowing his eyes.

"No, she's not," Maria said quickly. "Slade has told us all about his beloved Mattie. He's mighty eager to finish up here and get back to Dodge. Taking Becca will serve you no purpose, Henry, none at all."

"I don't believe you," Folger said, his voice rising. "Oh, you're clever, the two of you, but you're dealing with Henry Folger. I'm not a fool. I know a man who has staked a claim on a woman when I see one. Ironbow definitely considers Becca his. Enough talk. I want to be miles away before Ironbow discovers I've disappeared with his, shall we say, personal property."

Dear heaven, no, Becca screamed silently. She couldn't ride off into the darkness with the sick, evil man who had killed her father. Oh, where was Slade?

"Quickly," Folger said. "We'll go to the barn and get your horse, Becca. I'll leave Maria tied up out there. She can tell Ironbow just what happened to his precious Becca. Then we'll see who actually won."

"Henry," Maria said, "taking Becca away isn't going to give you back Four Aces. You lost—"

"Shut up!" he roared. "I had it all planned. The Bonnie Blue and Becca were to be mine. Mine!"

As he ranted on, Becca glanced at the rifle on the sofa. If she could just get that rifle. Once she and Maria left the house with Folger, there might not be any other chance of escape. She inched toward the sofa, but Folger abruptly jerked his attention back to her.

"Dammit, Becca, move. I'm not wasting any more time here." He gestured with his gun. "Go. Now!"

"All right, Henry," she said, "I'll go with you. Just give me your word that you won't hurt Maria. Surely the word of a Folger is still good. Or is it?"

"Of course it is," Folger said. "You insult me by even asking. Yes, you have my word that Maria won't be harmed if you do exactly as I say. Let's get going to the barn."

"Damn your hide, Henry Folger!" Maria suddenly cried. "You won't touch my Becca. I'll see you in hell first!"

She lunged for the rifle just as Slade appeared in the doorway, his gun drawn.

"Drop it, Folger," Slade ordered.

At the sound of Slade's voice, Folger spun around and pulled the trigger. The bullet slammed into Slade's left shoulder. He fell back against the wall as he fired his own gun.

"Damn you, Ironbow!" Folger yelled as the bullet exploded in his chest. "You won't have her. I won!"

Crumpling to the floor, he lifted his gun one last time. As Maria hefted the rifle and turned on him, he tried to hold the gun steady and fired. Maria fell forward onto the sofa as Folger died.

"Maria!" Becca screamed. She dropped to her knees and gently turned Maria onto her back. "Oh, Maria." A large bloodstain was spreading across the bodice of Maria's dress. "Don't move. I'll get bandages. Maria, you're going to be fine. I'll be right back."

"No, Becca," Maria said, grasping Becca's hand, "you must listen to me. Slade?"

He came forward, one hand clutching his shoulder, blood oozing between his fingers. "I'm here."

"I'm dying," Maria said.

"No," Becca whispered. "No, no."

Slade's gaze flickered over the rapidly growing blood-stain. "Yes."

"Dammit, Slade," Becca cried. "We've got to help her. We've got to do something."

"Hush, honey," Maria said, "and listen to me. Slade, tell Mattie I'm sorry if what I'm about to do is wrong, but I have to do what I think is right."

"I'll tell her," Slade said. A wave of dizziness swept over him and he sank onto a chair, tightening his hold on his shoulder.

"Becca," Maria said, her voice already growing weak, "Slade came here to pay a debt to Jed Colten for Mattie Muldoon. Mattie and I have been close for many, many years. I never met Slade before, but he told me that he and Mattie are friends, nothing more."

"You know Mattie Muldoon?" Becca asked, shocked. "Why didn't you tell me that before? No, this can all keep. We'll talk later. The important thing now is to tend to your wound."

"Becca, no, there's no time. I know I'm dying, and Slade knows it, too. You've got to accept that."

"No," Becca said, tears filling her eyes. "Don't leave me, Maria. I love you, I need you so much. Please, please, don't die."

"You're not alone, Becca. Slade is here with you. You sit down and talk to him woman to man. Both of you listen to the voices of your hearts, and see what you want for the future. And you have a family here on the Bonnie Blue. Frank, Yancey, so many others who care about you."

"Yes, but . . . I need you, my mother. I'll ride into Jubele—"

"No," Maria said. "Becca, you *have* a mother. It's time you knew the truth. Slade knows, and it isn't right that secrets be kept between a man and woman who love each other."

"It's time I knew what truth? Slade, what is she talking about?"

"Listen to her, Becca," he said. He grimaced as hot pain shot through his shoulder and down his arm. "This is her decision. She wants you to know."

Becca looked at Maria again. "All right. I'm listening, Maria."

"You're not alone, honey," Maria said, her eyes drifting closed. "So many people care about you, love you. And among them is . . . your mother. The woman who gave birth . . . to you. Your mother, Becca. Your . . . mother who loved you enough to . . . You still have a . . . mother. You still . . . have . . . Mattie."

"What?" Becca whispered. "You're saying that Mattie Muldoon is my mother? How can this be true? Maria?"

Slade pushed himself to his feet, shaking his head to clear it as a dark curtain threatened to drop over his senses. He looked down at Maria.

"She's gone, Becca," he said gently.

"No!" Becca cried, grasping Maria's hands. "No! Maria, wake up! Don't leave me!"

"Becca . . ."

She got shakily to her feet, tears streaming down her face. "Maria, my wonderful Maria . . ." Tears choked off her words, and she covered her face with her hands as sobs consumed her.

Slade nearly groaned aloud in frustration. He ached to pull Becca into his arms and comfort her. But he didn't dare remove his hand from the wound in his shoulder. He was losing blood rapidly, and he had to tend to that.

Becca lifted her head, tears still flowing down her cheeks. "Oh, God, Slade, I can't believe Maria is dead. My father, and now . . . I'm losing the people I love. I don't want Maria to be gone too. I don't know what to do."

"Becca, please try to ease your mind. Please, honey . . ."

She lifted a knitted afghan from the back of the sofa, then gently and carefully covered Maria's body. "I loved you so much, Maria." She looked at Slade again. "I'm tired. I think I should rest now."

"Yes, that's fine."

She frowned. "Is that blood on your shirt? No, it couldn't be. Maria was shot. There was blood . . . so much blood . . . I'm tired, Slade."

"Go rest, Becca." He didn't know what to do or say to help her! Maybe rest *was* the answer. "See if you can sleep for a while in your room."

"Yes."

He watched her drift from the room, his jaw tight with frustration. A minute later he walked unsteadily down the hall to the kitchen, each step sending a jarring pain through his shoulder. With a groan, he sank onto a chair at the table.

He couldn't think clearly. The loss of blood and the physical shock were taking a toll. He'd been no help to Becca at all, and could only pray that if she slept she'd awaken with a clearer mind. Then her questions would begin. How was he to explain about Mattie?

Brady Webster strode in the back door, bringing Slade from his troubled thoughts. "Got yourself shot from the looks of you, huh, Slade?"

"Yep. The bullet is still in there. Maria and Folger are dead. Becca's in some sort of shock. She's resting upstairs, but I'm worried about her."

"Well, let's get you tended to. Becca will be all right. I'm truly sorry about Maria. As for Folger, it's over. The Bonnie Blue men can move the Four Aces cattle over here whenever you're ready. As for the land, I can put it up for public auction, since there are no relatives to claim it. There's nobody in this area who can beat the Bonnie Blue on a bid. Four Aces and the Bonnie Blue together is going to be one helluva spread."

"Yep."

"And you wish I'd shut my mouth," Brady said, "and see about getting that bullet out of you. Let's get some whiskey in you, Slade, and numb you up a bit, then I'll go to work on you."

"Fine," Slade said, his mind centered on Becca. "Let's get it done."

The familiar smells of cooking and the sounds of children's laughter brought Slade from a deep sleep that had been plagued with nightmares and a strange, uncomfortable heat. He heard a man moaning, then realized the sound came from himself.

He tentatively opened his eyes to find that he was where he deduced he was: on the reservation with his father's people. But why was he there and, even more important, how long had he been there? Where was Becca?

He heard a door open, and a young Indian woman entered the room. Two thick braids of black hair fell over full breasts, clearly defined beneath the soft material of her dress. She carried a small wooden tray, and sank gracefully onto a chair beside his bed.

"Greetings, Slade Ironbow," she said in the language of their tribe. "It is good to see you free of the fever at last. I will change the bandage on your wound, then bring you food and drink."

"Greetings, Morning Mist. What fever do you speak of? How long have I been here?"

"Four days you have been with us, Slade. The white man's doctor was away, and everyone agreed we could tend to your wound much better here. The bullet was in very deep, and infection was starting. Your father and the others brought you back here. Your father will be pleased your fever has broken." She began to change the bandage on his shoulder. "You called for her, Slade. In your fever, you called her name many times. Becca."

"Do you know where—" Slade started to say, then stopped as a shadow fell over the doorway. "Father."

"Ah, my son is awake," Lone Eagle said, entering the room. "It is good that we brought you here. The Indian's medicine is much more powerful than the white man's."

"I might have been asked where I wished to be," Slade said, glaring at his father.

"I asked you," the chief said, all innocence, "but you were unconscious at the time and had no opinion to express. After your lovely Becca awakened from her healing sleep, I spoke with her and she agreed that since the white-man doctor from Jubele had been called away, your coming home with me was best, since the fever had struck you."

"Becca just shipped me off the Bonnie Blue?" Slade asked, attempting to sit up. He fell back, though, groaning and clutching his shoulder. "Damn."

"You stay still," Morning Mist said firmly. "If you start that wound bleeding again, I'll leave you to drown in your own blood." She stood. "I'll get you some food and drink now." She stomped out of the room.

"Drown in my own blood?" Slade muttered.

Lone Eagle chuckled and sat in the chair Morning Mist had vacated. As he gazed at his son, his smile faded.

"It is good to see your eyes clear, my son," he said, "and not clouded with the ghosts of the fever. Your skin burned for many days and nights."

"I have to get back to the Bonnie Blue, Father. Becca doesn't know of my love for her, nor do I know for certain how she feels about me. I must speak to her."

Lone Eagle nodded. "That would be wise, my son. Women left alone with their own thoughts are capable of devising great ills to create misery for the men who care for them. But it will be several days before you can attempt that ride. You lost much blood, Slade, and the fever took its toll. You must be patient a short time longer, then you can go to your Becca and speak what is in your heart."

"But—"

"Slade, I do not think that you wish to tell Morning Mist that you plan to sit on your horse for a hard ride before she declares you fit to do so."

"Well, I . . . No, I do not wish to encounter the wrath of Morning Mist."

"You are wise, Slade Ironbow," the chief said, nodding. "Women, it would seem, grow stronger with each new generation. Or, perhaps, it is only that I grow older and weaker."

"No, Father," Slade said dryly, "it is the women. They grow stronger in mind as well as body."

"So be it. You rest now, Slade. Morning Mist will be looking at my scalp if I tire you."

"Father, was everything taken care of at the Bonnie Blue?"

"That is fine land, Slade. The cattle from Four Aces were rebranded with the Bonnie Blue brand. Maria was buried in the family plot beneath big old trees. A man could grow old on the Bonnie Blue, Slade, find an inner peace there."

"Yep."

"A man could love well there."

"Yep."

"Raise fine sons."

"Yep."

Lone Eagle got to his feet. "I do not enjoy speaking with you when you sound like a man who knows few words of my language. I will tell Morning Mist to hurry with your food."

Slade sighed wearily as his father left the room, the effort of conversation making him more than ready for sleep. But he would eat first, and begin the process of regaining his strength. He wanted to return to the Bonnie Blue as quickly as possible. He wanted to see Becca, touch her, kiss her, speak to her. He had waited long enough. The time was now.

A week later, Slade sat on his horse high on the hill where he'd first seen the land of the Bonnie Blue stretching in all directions. Warmth swept through him, nudging aside his fatigue and the dull ache in his shoulder, and telling him he was, indeed, home. This was the Bonnie Blue, one of the finest ranches in all of Texas, and down there in that majestic house was Becca.

Yes, Slade Ironbow had come home.

He turned his horse and started down the hill.

An hour later he was finally approaching the house. Bucky was sweeping the wide front porch as the first streaks of the sunset were inching across the sky behind him. Bucky looked up at the sound of a horse and dropped the broom.

"Slade!" he yelled. "It's good to see you. You sure enough do look better than when they carted you out of here. We were hard-pressed to know if you were going to pull through. Your father sent word a couple of days ago that you were fine, and we were all mighty pleased to hear that."

"Thanks," Slade said, wondering if the boy was ever going to wind down. "Everything all right here?"

"Oh, you bet. Yes, sir, we're getting back to normal now, what with this trouble with Folger settled. Miss Becca, she bought the Four Aces land at the auction, and now she's got to decide just what all she intends to do with it. Yancey's been acting as foreman for now. We figured you'd be back, even though Miss Becca never said as much. We just figured you would, is all. And here you are . . . back on the Bonnie Blue. That's real fine, Slade, real fine."

"Thank you, Bucky."

"You ready for some supper? You're welcome in the bunkhouse, you know. Everyone will be mighty glad to see you."

"I'll be along, Bucky, but first thing I want to say hello to Miss Becca."

Bucky frowned. "But she isn't here. Didn't you know that? Well, no, how could you?"

Slade narrowed his eyes. "What do you mean she's not here? Where is she?"

"Well, see, she was mighty worried about you and the bad way you was when your father and those other Indians hauled you out of here. But then word came that you were going to be fine and all, and Miss Becca was washin' up her dresses and packin' things, and Yancey took her into Jubele this morning to catch the stage."

"Bucky," Slade said, striving for patience, "where did she go?"

"Oh. Well, she said she had important business to take care of. She said she had to see some woman 'bout something personal. Yep, that's what she said. Then she got on the stage and headed out for Dodge City, Kansas."

"Oh, hell," Slade said. "Just damn it straight to hell."

Seventeen

"Slade Ironbow is coming!" The young boy ran along the wooden sidewalk as fast as his spindly legs would carry him. "Slade Ironbow is coming into Dodge City. He's 'bout a mile out, just ridin' slow. Did you hear? This is it for Doc Willis. Slade Ironbow is back in Dodge."

Men and women who had been walking along the sidewalk stopped and whispered fiercely to one another. Store-keepers stepped outside and peered into the distance to see if they could get a glimpse of Slade. Excitement hummed in the air, enlivening the hot, dusty afternoon.

"Slade Ironbow is coming," the boy continued to yell as he ran. "Slade Ironbow is back in Dodge."

Doc turned from the half-opened window of Mattie's bedroom and smiled at her. She sat at her dressing table across the room brushing her hair, and caught his reflection in the mirror. She returned his smile, and he crossed the room to her, placing his hands on her shoulders.

"There's a lot of commotion down on the street," he said. "Did you hear what that boy was yelling?"

"No, I couldn't make out his words. What's going on out there?"

"Ma'am, the sidewalks are lined with people who wouldn't dream of missing what they've waited all this time for. Slade is about to ride into town."

Mattie jumped to her feet. "Slade's back? He's here in Dodge?"

"That's the big news being circulated along the street." He pulled his suit coat off the back of a chair and shrugged into it. "I'd best get down there."

"I'm going with you." Mattie smoothed the skirt of her pink cotton day dress over her hips. "Oh, Jim, do you realize what this probably means? Slade has solved the problems at the Bonnie Blue, taken care of the threat against Becca and the ranch." She suddenly frowned. "I was hoping that Becca and Slade would . . . Well, I should know by now that not all of my fantasies are going to come true."

Doc smiled, cradling her face in his hands. "My favorite fantasy *did* come true, Mattie Muldoon. You agreed to marry me, to be my wife for the rest of our lives. All we've been waiting for is Slade to get back in town so he can stand up with us as our witness." He chuckled. "Of course, those folks down there think that he'll have shot me dead before sundown. Poor souls. They're going to be mighty disappointed."

"Well, I refuse to have you get yourself shot just to satisfy the citizens of Dodge City. I intend to be a wife, not a widow."

"Perfect," he said, then lowered his head to give her a long, searing kiss. His breathing was rough when he raised his lips from hers. "Oh, Mattie, I love you so much."

"And I love you, Jim," she whispered.

"We'd better get downstairs and wait for Slade outside

the Spur." He smiled. "Let's follow his lead on handling the situation."

"All right."

"Then we'll make arrangements to be married."

"Jim, Abe has heard rumors that the preacher won't marry us because I'm . . . Well, it may be that we'll have to be married after we sell the Silver Spur and start on our way to California."

"The preacher is refusing to—We'll see about that. Anyway, that's to be tended to later. Let's go down and meet Slade. I certainly feel calm for a man who's about to get himself shot."

Their mingled laughter danced through the air as they left Mattie's room.

Slade pulled his Stetson low as he scrutinized the growing crowd along the main street of Dodge. An expectant hush followed him as he rode slowly toward the Silver Spur.

He knew these people were figuring he'd discover that Doc Willis was spending time with Mattie Muldoon. Now he was back and would shoot the doctor deader than yesterday.

He smiled thinly. He was bone-weary and hungry, and his shoulder was aching, but he would have to attend to this business with Doc before he could get any rest. This was not going to go the way the proper but bloodthirsty citizens of Dodge City were anticipating.

As he approached the Silver Spur, Mattie and Doc stepped outside. A collective gasp went up from the attentive audience as Doc slid his arm around Mattie's shoulders and tucked her close to his side.

Abe ambled out of the saloon and settled on a wooden bench. The girls peered cautiously over and under the half-doors.

Slade stopped in front of the Spur and swung out of the saddle, dropping his horse's reins to the ground. He stood about ten feet back from the sidewalk and hooked his thumbs in the front of his gun belt.

Never had a town that size become so quiet so quickly.

"Well, now, this is interesting," he said, his gaze flickering over Mattie and Doc.

"This is the way it is, Slade," Doc said in a loud voice. "Mattie is my woman now. She's going to become my wife."

A murmur went up from the crowd.

"Here comes trouble," Abe said, shaking his head. "Mighty big trouble."

"I refused to marry them," a voice called shakily. "Place no blame on me, Mr. Ironbow. I won't be a party to this union."

Slade looked over the throng until he found the round face of the preacher. "You're saying you refuse to make this couple husband and wife, Preacher Bolstad?"

"Oh, I surely won't marry 'em, Mr. Ironbow," the obviously nervous man said. "No, sir, I won't do it. You got no cause to find fault with me, Mr. Ironbow. No cause at all."

Slade gazed at Preacher Bolstad for a long moment, then turned back to Mattie and Doc.

"Well," he said, "the truth is, I'm tired, I'm hungry, and I'd like to get this over with."

"That's fine with me, Slade," Doc said.

"You're telling me, Doc," Slade said, "that Mattie is your woman now." Doc nodded. "Mattie," Slade went on, "did you plan on wearing a fancy dress to marry Doc?"

"No, not really," she said. "That part isn't important to me."

"Preacher Bolstad," Slade said loudly, "I'd like to see your prayer book, if I may."

"Oh, yes, of course," the fidgety man said. "Amen to

that. Yes, of course. Here, someone pass this over to Mr. Ironbow."

Slade flipped through the prayer book until he found the page he wanted, then he reached into one of his saddlebags and drew out a small, flat leather case. Silence fell over Dodge once again as he walked over to Mattie and Doc.

"This badge," he said, opening the leather case, "will identify me as a Special Federal Marshal, operating on selected cases by order of the President."

"What?" Mattie whispered.

"Now *that* makes sense," Doc said. "That's where you go when you disappear."

"Well, well, well," Abe said.

A buzz of opinion hummed from the crowd.

"Along with other authority," Slade went on, "I'm capable of acting as Justice of the Peace when called upon to do so. I, therefore, will unite this man and this woman in holy matrimony." His gaze swept over the crowd. "They have my blessings. If you don't approve, then go. If you choose to be a witness to this celebration, you're welcome to stay."

"Well, I do declare," a woman exclaimed, then grabbed her husband's arm and hauled him off down the sidewalk.

A dozen others also left, glaring at the bride and groom before stomping away, but the remainder of the people stayed right where they were.

"Wait! Wait!" Widow Sullivan called as she came thundering down the sidewalk. "Mercy, I'm breathing my last," she gasped, stopping by Mattie and Doc. "No bride is a bride without flowers and a veil." She handed Mattie a small bouquet, then settled a frothy veil on her head.

Mattie smiled. "Thank you, Widow Sullivan. Thank you so much."

"Now, *Reverend* Ironbow," Widow Sullivan said, "you may proceed."

So, there in front of the Silver Spur saloon in Dodge City, Kansas, Special Marshal Slade Ironbow, the dust of the trail on his clothes and a smile on his face, spoke the words that declared Mattie Muldoon the wife of James Willis. When the groom kissed the bride, a cheer went up from the crowd.

"Well, now ain't that something?" Abe said. "I think that is mighty, mighty fine."

"Oh-h-h," Clara said, sniffling. "That was the most beautiful thing I ever did see."

"I love you, Mattie," Jim whispered to her.

"I love you, Jim, and I always will." She turned to the crowd. "Come into the Spur. Drinks are on the house, and there's sweet tea for the ladies. Everyone is welcome."

"Don't mind if I do," Widow Sullivan said, bustling through the saloon doors.

Mattie turned to Slade. "Slade . . ." She smiled. "Or is it Marshal Ironbow? I want a hug from you."

"I'll get your dress dirty, Mattie," he said, and kissed her on the cheek. "I'm happy for you both."

"What's wrong?" Mattie asked. "I've had hugs from you before when you've been trail-dirty, Slade Ironbow. What aren't you telling me?"

"There's a thick bandage on his left shoulder," Doc said quietly. "One of your hugs would be a bit painful at the moment, I imagine."

"Slade?"

"It's all right, Mattie. The bandage needs changing, and I have to wash up. I'll go to the hotel now. Doc, would you come over in a bit and see to the bandage?"

Doc nodded as Mattie asked, "But what about Becca? How is she?"

"Come to the hotel in one hour, Mattie. I'll buy you two a wedding supper and tell you everything."

"All right," she said. "But what happened—"

Doc gave her a quick kiss. "One hour. Go on inside.

There's a party at the Spur, remember? Come on, Slade, you're looking a bit gray around the edges. I'll go with you now and take a look at that shoulder."

"But how . . ." Mattie began, but the two men had started away with Slade's horse in tow.

Much later, Slade, Mattie, and Doc sat in a secluded corner of the dining room at the hotel, finishing their supper. Slade had managed to eat while telling the other two what had transpired at the Bonnie Blue.

"Dear heaven," Mattie said after he told them about Becca's journey, "Becca's coming here to Dodge City because of what Maria said before she died? Becca is coming looking for me?"

Slade nodded. "I caught up with the stage early this morning. She's definitely on it. She'll be here tomorrow." Sadness briefly shadowed his eyes. "She doesn't know I'm here, so it's not me she's after."

Doc studied him. "Although you wish it were."

Slade frowned. "I didn't say that."

"You didn't have to," Doc said. "I've been on that path, Slade." He smiled at Mattie. "It's lonely and it hurts, but there are times when it works out, too. I wish you well."

"Are you in love with Becca?" Mattie asked.

"Well, I . . ." Slade shifted uncomfortably. "I . . . That's not the subject at hand. We're discussing the fact that Becca's arriving tomorrow to find her real mother. You."

"Oh, Lord," Mattie said, the color draining from her face. "What am I going to say to her?"

"The truth," Slade said. "It's time for the truth, Mattie."

"What about you, Slade?" she asked. "Are you going to tell Becca how you really feel about her?"

Slade stood up. "I need some sleep. Be happy, Dr. and Mrs. Willis. I guess we disappointed some folks today, having a wedding instead of a shooting, but I think most everyone is pleased for you."

"Slade, wait a minute," Mattie said, catching his arm. "I've always ignored the wild rumors about you, and now it turns out that you're actually a Federal Marshal."

He nodded. "I have been for several years, mediating between the officials in Washington and some of the more reluctant Indian chiefs who were resisting the white man's laws. I'm about ready to turn in this badge, though, because there's no need for my help any longer."

"You make a fine preacher," Doc said, chuckling.

"Thanks," Slade said dryly. "I'll talk to you tomorrow. Good night."

"Good night," Mattie and Doc said in unison, watching him leave the dining room.

"We'll be in Dodge City 'bout a half-hour from now," an old cowboy said to Becca. "Surely will be glad to set my feet on solid ground. Ain't never ridin' in one of these here stagecoach things again. No, sir, this is enough for me."

Becca smiled and nodded absently. Dodge City, she thought. Oh, Lord, she was nervous. She was going to find and speak to her mother, Mattie Muldoon. If only Slade were there with her. But Slade was recuperating on the Indian reservation.

The questions that had plagued her for two weeks whirled through her head. If Mattie Muldoon was, indeed, her mother, why had she been raised on the Bonnie Blue and told she was Bonnie and Jed Colten's daughter? Why had Slade contacted Mattie Muldoon at a saloon? So many questions.

"Dodge City!" the stagecoach driver yelled. "Five more minutes, folks."

"Praise the Lord," the old cowboy muttered.

Becca clutched her hands tightly in her lap to hide their trembling.

No one in Dodge questioned the arrival of an attractive young woman, traveling alone on the stagecoach. Nor were eyebrows raised when she checked into the hotel. Women were beginning to exhibit their independence.

There were, however, three people who were very aware that Becca Colten was in town—Slade, Mattie, and Doc. From Mattie's upstairs window, they had watched Becca's arrival.

"I can't see her face clearly from here," Mattie said. "Is she pretty, Slade?"

"Yes," he said quietly, still looking out the window, although Becca was inside the hotel. "She's very beautiful."

Doc touched Mattie's arm and shook his head, indicating she shouldn't say any more. The three were silent, lost in their own thoughts.

Eighteen

By late afternoon, Becca had run out of excuses to keep from seeking out Mattie Muldoon. She was disgusted with her lack of courage, and stood in front of the mirror in her hotel room for one last inspection. Her parasol matched her mint-green dress; her soft kid boots were unsmudged and her white gloves were spotless.

She was Becca Colten, she told herself, lifting her chin. Coltens didn't turn tail and run from anything. She didn't care what anyone said about who she was or who her mother was. She had been raised with Colten strength and pride.

She picked up her reticule and left the room. She would ignore, she decided firmly, the butterflies swooshing in her stomach, and the yearning to have Slade Ironbow miraculously appear before her. She was Becca Colten, going in search of the woman who was her mother, if in name only.

When Becca reached the bottom of the stairs, the hotel clerk called her over.

"Yes?" Becca asked.

"Miss Colten, Doc Willis says he'd appreciate it if you could spare him a minute. He's waiting for you in the front parlor there."

Becca shook her head. "I'm afraid he must have the wrong person. I don't know anyone by that name."

"Well, he sure enough does know you."

"I'll step into the parlor and correct the error." She smiled. "Thank you."

Doc got to his feet as soon as Becca entered the nicely furnished room. Noting the confused expression on her face, he quickly crossed the parlor to her.

"Miss Colten," he said, smiling, "this is a pleasure."

"I'm afraid you have me at a disadvantage, Dr. Willis. I don't recall having met you."

"We haven't met, Miss Colten, although I feel as though I've known you for a long time. Please . . ." He swept one arm in the direction of some overstuffed chairs. "May we sit down for a few minutes?"

"All right."

She sat in a green print chair, and Doc sat opposite her. He gazed at her for so long, she frowned.

"Is something wrong, Dr. Willis?"

"What? Oh, no, not at all. Staring at you like that was rude. Forgive me, please, but I can see the resemblance between you and Mattie clearly."

Becca stiffened. "How do you know about my relationship with—with Mattie Muldoon?"

"She told me. You see, her name is actually Mattie Willis now, because she and I are married. We plan to start a new life together in California once we sell her saloon, the Silver Spur. We knew you were coming to Dodge City to see Mattie, and she sent me here to the hotel to speak with you first."

"You knew I was coming? But how? Unless—" Becca's eyes widened. "Is Slade in Dodge City? I assumed he was still with his father. Are you saying that Slade Ironbow knows I'm here, and has made no attempt to contact me?"

"Miss Colten," Doc said, looking down, "I don't intend to get involved in your personal business with Slade." Glancing at her again, he chuckled. "I don't envy the man, either, when you catch up with him. Your eyes flash just like Mattie's when you're angry." His smile faded. "Mattie is why I'm here. She's concerned for you, because she'd do nothing to cast a shadow over your reputation. She thought you might prefer to arrange to meet somewhere other than the Spur."

"Oh, I see," Becca said quietly. "That was very considerate of her." She got to her feet. "However, I'm not one for subterfuge. I'm going calling on Mattie Muldoon . . . Mattie Willis, and it's no one's business as to why. I'd appreciate your escorting me to the Silver Spur, Dr. Willis, if you'd be so kind."

"I'd be honored," he said, offering her his arm. "Oh, you are your mother's daughter. Yes, I'm truly honored."

"Thank you. One question, Dr. Willis. Is Slade in Dodge City? You were cleverly evasive before, but I'd like a direct answer."

"Well . . ."

"Doctor?"

"Your mother's daughter," he said, shaking his head. "Yes, Slade is here. Miss Colten . . . Becca, don't judge him too harshly. He feels the important issue at the moment is you and Mattie."

"Shall we go?" Becca said stiffly.

"Oh, Lord," Doc murmured, rolling his eyes heavenward.

The butterflies in Becca's stomach whirled in agitation as she walked with Dr. Willis toward the Silver Spur. Mattie Muldoon Willis, her mother, was in that building. And Slade was in town, and was staying away from her.

Well, she deserved better than that. Slade had said they were going to talk, and like it or not, they were going to talk.

"Here we are," Doc said, pulling Becca from her tangled thoughts. "Once we're inside, we'll go straight up the stairs to Mattie's rooms. Ready?"

She hesitated only a moment. "Yes."

The Silver Spur was busy and noisy, but the appearance of a young lady on Doc Willis's arm cast a hush over the crowd of men. Everyone watched as the pair went directly up the stairs and on to Mattie's rooms. Doc took a key from his pocket and unlocked the door to the office. When they'd disappeared inside, the noise in the saloon increased tenfold as the men speculated loudly about what they'd just seen.

Upstairs, Doc led Becca across the sparsely furnished office. He smiled encouragingly at Becca, knocked lightly on the sitting room door, then turned the knob and pushed it open.

"Mattie," he called as he and Becca entered. "Mattie?"

Mattie appeared in the bedroom doorway and walked slowly into the sitting room, her gaze locked on Becca. Becca met her gaze, but neither spoke.

"I think," Doc said, breaking the heavy silence, "that I'll leave you two alone now. I'll be downstairs if you need me. All right?"

Both women remained silent, and Doc quickly backed out of the room.

"Becca," Mattie said at last, "would you care to sit down? I have so much to tell you. But first, let me say how sorry I am about Jed Colten and Maria. You've endured so much, and my heart aches for you. I'm glad that at least Slade was there during the worst of the trouble."

"Yes, he was at the Bonnie Blue," Becca said stiffly, "but that's another matter. I'm very eager to hear the truth about who I really am." She sat down on a chair, and looked up at Mattie. "This is so difficult," she said softly. "I can see myself in you, but to suddenly learn that Bonnie Colten wasn't my mother, and that you are, is like telling me I've never been who I thought I was."

Mattie sat down in the chair next to hers, resisting the urge to take her daughter's hand.

"Becca, let me start at the beginning. I promise every word will be the truth, with no details left out. You can then judge what I did and why I did it. I ask only that you listen to me before you pass judgment."

Becca nodded, and Mattie began her story.

When she was through, tears filled both women's eyes.

"Becca," Mattie said, her voice husky, "from what Slade told me about you and what I can see in you myself, I'm proud to be your mother. But that's not the point. I'll—I'll understand if you walk out of here and pretend this meeting never took place. There's no pride for you in knowing your mother runs a house of pleasure."

Becca slowly stood and crossed the room to look out of the window. Below, an enchanting swing hung from a huge old tree. After a moment she turned to meet Mattie's gaze.

"I think," she said, "that I am blessed to have a mother who loved me enough, and had enough strength, to give me a chance at the kind of life Jed Colten could offer me. How could I feel anything but pride in knowing I'm your daughter?"

Mattie got to her feet. "Oh, Becca," she said, opening her arms. "Oh, my darling child, thank you."

Becca went into Mattie's embrace unhesitantly. It felt right, warm and comforting. They held each other tightly, then sat down again, hands entwined, and talked. They laughed and shared, and began to fill in the missing years of their lives.

*   *   *

"It's past supper hour," Doc said to Slade. "Mattie and Becca have been upstairs for hours."

"Yep."

"I sure hope this means they're getting on well together."

"Yep."

"The Silver Spur is filling up. I don't suppose we should be taking this table away from paying customers, but I'm not budging until Mattie and Becca come down those stairs."

"No."

"Dammit, Slade, say more then 'yep' and 'no.' These hours have been agony for me."

Slade leaned forward to rest his arms on the table. "Doc," he said quietly, his gaze still fixed on the stairs, "I've been sitting here looking at my life, sort of like you did on your birthday, and I know one thing for sure."

"Which is?"

"Before this night ends, Becca Colten will have agreed to be my wife."

Doc grinned. "I'll be damned. Married? You?"

"Yep."

"Whoa. Don't go back to 'yep' and 'no.' Do you think Becca's going to give you any fuss about getting married? I had one rough road to go with that Mattie Muldoon, I'll tell you. What do you think Becca's going to say or do?"

Slade chuckled. "If I could understand the workings of a woman's mind, I'd be the richest man on earth. I don't know what Becca will say, but I do know that I love her. I'm fairly certain she loves me, and I have no intention of spending the rest of my life with only the wind."

"I'll be damned," Doc said again. "Good luck, Slade. You'll need it, because Becca is definitely Mattie's daughter. They have a stubborn streak in them, those two, and a temper—" Doc abruptly straightened in his chair. "Slade, Mattie and Becca just came out of Mattie's office."

Slade sat back in his chair again, his arms crossed

over his chest. Though he looked half-asleep, he was quite aware of Becca descending the stairs with Mattie.

"They're smiling," Doc said out of the corner of his mouth.

"Mmm," Slade said.

"It's getting very quiet in here, Slade, just like when I brought Becca in. Everyone is staring at them."

"Let's just hope," Slade said in his coldest voice, "these cowboys have brains enough not to touch who they're looking at."

"I'd best get back to the hotel," Becca said as she reached the bottom step. "The time just slipped away from us."

"It was time wonderfully spent. Becca, have supper with Jim and me. He's in here somewhere. Goodness, you're being stared at, my beautiful girl, and you could hear a pin drop in here. There's Jim. He's at that back table against the wall. He's—Oh. Well, maybe we should meet you at the hotel in a bit."

Frowning, Becca gazed across the room at Jim Willis. Her eyes narrowed when she saw who was sitting with him.

"I do believe," she said, "that I'll have a word with Mr. Ironbow."

"Becca," Mattie whispered, "this isn't the time. The Spur is a man's place. You shouldn't even be in here, let alone go strolling all the way across the saloon. You don't look like a Silver Spur girl, but these boys will surely think you are if you stay. Speak with Slade later. I'm certain you two can talk through your differences, but this isn't the place!"

"It will do just fine," Becca said, and started across the quiet, crowded room.

"Oh my Lord," Mattie whispered.

•　　•　　•

"Slade," Doc muttered, "are you awake? Becca is coming over here, and she looks like a brewing storm." He stood up hurriedly. "I'm going to go check on my wife. Good luck."

Slade didn't move as Becca came closer. Though his heart beat wildly, he forced himself to remain motionless.

At last she reached his table.

"Mr. Ironbow," she said coolly.

"Miss Colten."

"I'd like to speak to you."

He didn't move. He wanted to decide himself when and where they'd have a serious discussion, and it certainly wouldn't be in a saloon filled with cowboys.

"Mr. Ironbow," she said, "you're being rude."

"If you want to speak, Miss Colten, you go right ahead."

She glanced around. "Don't be ridiculous."

He lifted one shoulder in a shrug. "Then I suppose we'll have to talk later, when I'm ready to leave the Spur."

She was going to kill this man, Becca thought. She loved him with every breath in her body, and she had every intention of strangling him with her bare hands. They would talk when *he* was ready? The hell with that!

She took a deep breath, let it out, then said calmly, "Talking later isn't convenient for me. So, audience and all, I guess I'll simply have to speak my mind right here."

Slade tensed, but still didn't look up at her.

"Slade Ironbow," she went on, raising her voice enough so everyone could hear her, "I am in love with you. I will be in love with you until I am no longer breathing. I have every intention of marrying you and filling the Bonnie Blue ranch house with the sounds of your sons' laughter."

"Lawsy me," Abe muttered, "I ain't never heard no woman speak to Slade Ironbow like that."

" 'Bout time one did," Clara said. "I just wish it would have been me."

"Slade," Becca continued, "though you appear to be half-dead, half-drunk, or half-asleep, I know better. As a matter of fact, I know all kinds of wonderful, fascinating things about you. As your wife, of course, I would keep silent about all and everything, but as just another of your women?" She sighed dramatically. "I shall tell everyone about you, and live off my memories."

With great deliberation, Slade unfolded his arms, pressed his hands on his thighs, and stood. All of the men in the Spur seemed to make themselves smaller, not wanting to be in Slade Ironbow's way. There wasn't a sound in the huge room.

Slade pushed his Stetson back. His eyes met Becca's, and several long seconds passed in silence.

Then Slade reached into his shirt pocket and withdrew the thin leather case. He flipped it open in front of Becca's nose.

"Special Federal Marshal Slade Ironbow at your service, ma'am. Part of my responsibility to the President is to maintain top secrecy in all matters. Since I can't be certain just what you propose to tell this group of men, you leave me little choice, Becca Colten."

"Don't shoot her!" Clara screamed. "Don't shoot her, Slade!"

"Clara," Abe said, "would you kindly shut your mouth?"

"Let's go," Slade said, jerking his head at Becca.

"No. I refuse to leave here until you declare your intentions in front of these witnesses."

Mattie covered her eyes with one hand. Doc patted her arm.

"You're pushing me, Becca," Slade said, his jaw tightening.

"You'll get used to me in the thirty or forty years we'll have together." She paused, and her voice had softened when she spoke again. "Oh, Slade, I love you so much."

"The marshal in me dictates that I keep you quiet at all costs." He stepped closer to her. "The man in me simply says I'd be a fool not to keep you." He stroked one thumb over her lips. She shivered. "I love you, Becca. Marry me. I want you to be my wife."

There was definitely no one breathing in the Silver Spur saloon.

"Oh, yes," she said, flinging her arms around his neck. "Yes, yes, yes. I'll marry you, Slade."

Bedlam erupted. Mattie and all the Silver Spur girls wept. Abe poured drinks on the house, and the piano player thundered on the keys. Cowboys joined together to sing terribly off-key to help celebrate the pending marriage of Becca Colten and Slade Ironbow.

No one noticed that Becca and Slade were no longer in the Spur.

In Slade's hotel room they made sweet, slow love for hours, then talked, sharing their hopes and dreams for the lifetime they would spend together on the Bonnie Blue.

At last they slept, only to be awakened by a sudden noise that brought Slade rolling to his feet, wide-awake.

"What was it?" Becca asked sleepily when Slade returned to the bed.

He pulled her close, his hand skimming along her soft body. "Only the wind," he said, lowering his lips to hers, "saying good-bye."

Coming next month . . .

TEXAS! CHASE by Sandra Brown

Sandra Brown's wonderfully written romances always combine tender, unforgettable emotion with breathtaking sensuality. Her books consistently receive rave reviews from critics and fans alike. Sandra's second book in the Tyler family trilogy features Chase, who is attempting to recover from a terrible tragedy—the death of his beloved wife, Tanya, in an automobile accident and the loss of their unborn child. In anticipation of the child's birth, Chase and his wife had signed a contract to purchase a house. Tanya was a passenger in the realtor's, Marcie Johns's, car when the accident occurred.

Chase's grieving has affected his outlook on life, his work, and his relationship with his family. Complicating events even more for Chase is his growing attraction for Marcie—intensifying his guilt over losing his wife. In this excerpt, Chase and Marcie meet for the first time since the accident. Chase has been thrown from a bull while riding in a rodeo, and Marcie has come to the hospital to see if she can help him in some way.

For the first time in two years, she gazed into Chase Tyler's face. The last time she had looked into it, their positions had been reversed. She'd been lying semiconscious in a hospital bed and he had been standing beside it, weeping over his wife's accidental death.

A few months after that, Chase had left Milton Point for parts unknown. Word around town was that he was running the rodeo circuit, much to the distress of his family.

But now, as Marcie gazed into his face, which looked tormented even in repose, she wondered if he did hold her responsible for his beloved Tanya's death.

"Chase," she whispered sorrowfully.

He didn't stir, and his breathing was deep and even, indicating that the drug he had been given intravenously was working. Giving in to the desire she'd felt while lying in pain in her own hospital bed, Marcie gingerly ran her fingers through his dark hair, brushing back wavy strands that had fallen over his clammy forehead.

Even though he looked markedly older, he was still the most handsome man she'd ever seen. She had thought so the first day of kindergarten. She distinctly remembered Miss Kincannon's calling on him to introduce himself to the rest of the class and how proudly he had stood up and spoken his name. Marcie had been smitten. In all the years since, nothing had changed.

The mischievous, dark-haired little boy with the light-gray eyes, who had possessed outstanding leadership qualities and athletic prowess, had turned into quite a man. There was strength in his face and a stubborn pride in his square chin that bordered on belligerence, inherent, it seemed, to the Tyler men. They were noted for their quick tempers and willingness to stand up for themselves. Chase's lower jaw bore a dark-purple bruise now. Marcie shuddered to think how close he had come to having his skull crushed.

She noticed his hand moving restlessly over the tight bandage around his rib cage. Afraid he might hurt himself, she captured his hand and drew it down to his side, patting it into place beside his hip and holding it there.

His eyes fluttered open. Obviously disoriented, he blinked several times in an attempt to get his bearings and remember where he was.

Then he seemed to recognize her. Reassuringly, she closed her fingers tightly around his. He tried to speak, but the single word came out as nothing more than a faint croak.

Still, she recognized his pet name for her. Right before drifting back into oblivion he had said, "Goosey?"